RAVENOUS DESIRES

EROTIC SHORT STORIES, SECOND COLLECTION

JAMES GREY

CONTENTS

NOTE TO READERS

This collection contains three stand-alone stories and one for which background reading is recommended. In order to be prepared for *Hot Wet Touches Part II* at the end of this book, read the first part of the story in my first anthology: *Breaking Free*. It's available as both eBook and paperback. Alternatively, the full *Hot Wet Touches* novella is available as a standalone eBook.

For all the relevant links visit jamesgreyauthor.com.

And the raven, never flitting, still is sitting, still is
sitting
On the pallid bust of Pallas just above my chamber
door;
And his eyes have all the seeming of a demon's that is
dreaming,
And the lamp-light o'er him streaming throws his
shadow on the floor;
And my soul from out that shadow that lies floating on
the floor
Shall be lifted — nevermore!

From *The Raven* by Edgar Allan Poe

THE RAVEN

My pulse clicks up another gear. Right now is when the evening really begins. The facts are these. Dinner is done. It's only nine o'clock. I am walking in Oxford, England, with a delectable blonde. And I am smiling like crazy.

I've slain the idea that she's way out of my league. The nagging doubt. The urge to slink off into the darkness and leave her to the alphas. It's going too well for that. We're on our second date!

Yes, I do believe it's a date. We never said it in so many words, but my texts to her have been unequivocal. She knows why I am here, and she has come to me, looking better than ever. Make-up, dark eye shadow, perfume…the works. This feels a *lot* like a date. It's why I am smiling, and every breath of evening cool is so sweet.

It's an autumn night. Not freezing, like a true English winter's eve, but we can feel an edge in the air. She wants to walk, my little creature of the moonlight! Well, then, so do I.

Okay, I wanted her to drink more, too, because that never hurts, right? But it looks like she's decided to go easy on the alcohol tonight. Smart girl. She won't be *easy*, but I don't need her to be. She is worth any wait. So I went with it, and we plunged out of the pub, into the ancient streets.

Walking is what we do, she and I! We walked moments after we first met, three weeks ago, after I got talking to her at a photography exhibition. I'd used the dumbest of dumb lines. Words about her being from Finland, because, you know, the photographer was Finnish and, you know, she was the purest Scando blonde. Godawful words!

She wasn't even Scandinavian. Polish.

Wore a lot of black, I noticed.

But she smiled as she corrected my blundering chat-up, and then we talked like old friends. It wasn't one-way traffic. She wanted to know about *my* life too! And then, spontaneously — just like that! — we walked. Miles. Until night fell, and she let me have her number.

When we met up the next weekend, we walked again. More miles. More hours. We walked on Port Meadow, the marshy common land beyond the town. Port Meadow, with its cows, and its ducks, and its horses.

She taught me all the Polish words for the animals, and there it was, my nickname for her: *kaczuszka*. Little duck. *Kah-choosh-kah*. So perfectly right for this slight little creature, with her jet-black plumage. Just eighteen, she would barely make a ripple in water. Just like a *kaczuszka*. And she giggled every time I said it, failing so bad at the Polish. Which made me want to say it all the time.

So on Port Meadow we walked and walked, and then we sat on a tiny piece of log, inexplicably present in the middle of the vast, open lands. It was made for two beginner lovers, that little chunk of dead wood. Only by sitting shoulder to shoulder could two of you squeeze onto it.

We sat for an eternity, our sleeves touching with ease. She smoked her slim, long cigarettes, like a seasoned heroine in a black-and-white French film. Black clothes, white hair. She was made for monochrome.

Then a brown cow, eyes dark and benevolent, came over to greet us. Apprehensive, we scratched her nose and my *kaczuszka* squealed with glee. The worldly, hard-smoking adult was a child again.

Darkness came, and so too the chill. We laughed as she felt my hand, how cold it was. I lifted her over a stile — how light she was! We came to spooky, inky woods, and I thought to take her hand. But I didn't want to scare her. So I didn't take her hand. We paused on the bridge, by the houseboats, and looked at the stars. Then the fog came down, and we were alone in it. Perfectly alone.

And I grew more and more bewitched by this calm, intelligent and precious creature with the pale blue gem stone eyes. She who could walk around a field for all those hours. Just talking. Just enjoying our time. I was learning scraps of her language, and she was perfecting mine. Sometimes, for fun, we lapsed into the French both of us had studied.

Sometimes her thoughts were dark, but making her smile was all I wanted. Seeing her smile made my heart dance.

So now we're walking again. In the middle of town, this time. We have no plan, only the serpentine streets and lanes of the old university town. Spontaneous is good. But I need to kiss her tonight.

I need to take this connection of ours to the next level. I can go with the flow, but if my moment comes — that perfect cocktail of place and time — I must seize it. Before someone else does. Or before our moment passes. The mere thought sends a flood of dread into my veins.

The thought passes. I just know that moment will come tonight. I've felt like we've been in a movie since the moment our paths crossed that random Friday afternoon. The script says our time is tonight. I have a feeling in my gut that this night will change my life. It's not a feeling I want to shake.

Something else crosses my mind as we meander onto the red-brick square of Gloucester Green. She mentioned a guy the last time. Just once. Oh, only in the vaguest, most casual terms. He's in Portugal, and it's nothing official. It might be something, or nothing. She was just waiting and seeing. Long-distance was difficult, she said. And she shrugged her black, fur-coated shoulders a lot.

I have no qualms about disrupting this thing, if she is so clearly undecided as to its merits. Mr Nice Guy has retired! After all, I've recently concluded that there is no such thing as a truly single woman. There's always some guy, somewhere. Even if he's long gone and remains only in her head. You'll always have to push someone aside to get into a girl's heart. That's just how it is.

But it does make my assignment more difficult. I have fallen so hard for her that I will push through any barriers. I have a suspicion that she'll put some up for me. It just depends how many. Right now, she looks carefree and cool as she sucks on a roll-up. (She switched to them this week, because they take more effort. 'I'm lazy, so it means I'll smoke less.') But I'm sure her mind must be racing too. And I doubt her thoughts are as simple as mine.

My fawning smile floods back as I look at her once more. Smoking — that's *unattractive*. Period. Only, with her, I don't care. I'd almost be disappointed if she stopped. It's part of her aura. When we ate our pizza, she talked about how she liked the smell of smoke on her fingers before she goes to sleep. And now I want to smell her sweet little fingers.

She sees my inane grin, and she blesses me with a little smile too, before she glances awkwardly at the ground. Nerves? Doubts? Who could say? But for the thirtieth time my mind takes a snapshot of this perfect face, lips as red as cherries straight from the tree, so full and so kissable, corners turned up in happiness just the way I like them.

Her skin is pale as the blossom from that self-same cherry tree. She's been born with a melanin deficiency, and you know what? It works. I'm walking with a modern-day Snow White`1

[*The typing error above reminds us that at this exact moment in writing his first draft, the author was suddenly, distressingly interrupted. Three days passed before he continued below.*]

So, where was I? Let me rewind a moment. Take myself back to that magic night, pregnant with possibility.

Ah yes, we're strolling. Our destination? Nowhere in particular. She has broken out some white clothing for me tonight, rather than going for the head-to-toe black she so enjoys. She looked like a polished raven last time I saw her. Though she confided that she did own colourful red pyjamas. I didn't hear what she said after that. I was in bed with her, holding her warm, vulnerable little body tight and close. My precious treasure in red pyjamas, safe with me, always.

This evening, though, only the inky fur coat and dark trousers remain from my little French-speaker's *collection noire*. Her shoes are bright white for our date, and she has dug out a white t-shirt too. With black polka dots, naturally.

I had tried wearing black, to match what I'd thought she'd wear. I thought it might be romantic, but the outfit didn't work and I'd scrapped it in favour of jeans and a colourful shirt, mostly autumnal reds.

At dinner, we laughed about how we'd picked out our clothing. And all I could think was, *you could wear sack-cloth, sweetie, and your eyes would still be nectar enough for me.* And I'm thinking it now again. There is nowhere I would rather be.

"You're going to have to excuse me just a minute, Sir, but I'm going to talk to your Missus," says a voice in the dark.

We both jump. He's materialised from nowhere.

"I'm going to ask her for a roll-up, if you won't mind, guv'nor!"

There's a twinkle in his eye and a likeable note in his voice. But his face is grimy. He bears the scars of the streets. Also, there's a mostly empty bottle of white wine in his hand. We're being accosted by one of Oxford's many hoboes. Our stroll is taking an unexpected twist.

My instinct is to protect her, and I edge closer. But this guy is harmless. And there are plenty of people around. She's cool with it — grown up beyond her years — even though he disarms her of her own smouldering roll-up and finishes it himself. Outrageous, but done in such a way that you had to chuckle.

"You two are going to have beautiful children," he babbles. "Where are you from, love? Denmark? Sweden?"

"She's from Finland," I chime in, knowing she'll get the reference. She plays along. And of the fact that we're by no means a couple...she says nothing. I *like* that! But she does correct him on the kids question. She definitely doesn't want any. I knew that already. Just another thing we agree on.

"Oh, never say never," our new friend says, while she tries to roll him another smoke with her shaky fingers. She's still clumsy at the roll-up game. "Children are the greatest blessing you can have. Look."

And he fishes out a keyring. On it, a photo of a boy just a few months old. "That's my lad," he says with feeling, almost in tears. "He's my world. It's the best thing that could happen to the two of you. Mark my words." He kisses the picture with a dramatic flourish, and then he looks to the sky.

I glance at his bottle of wine, and find it hard to believe he's seen that child any time recently. And yet, his sentiment seems to come from the heart. That, or he's a good actor.

I decide to play along. "Let's wait till we're married, first, shall we?" I say, smiling at my *kaczuszka*. I slip my arm around her shoulder. Play-acting. It's just a game for now. Isn't it?

"You never know, mate," says our hobo. "One little accident, one night of passion…"

"Yeah, maybe tonight, huh?" my beautiful companion chimes in. She's playing along too. *Oh…please don't joke about things like that, my darling.* But I pull her a little closer.

He's street smart, of course, and he's now picked up that our relationship is seriously fresh. And he's doing his bit for me. "You're meant to be together," he rambles with conviction. "I can just see it. It's right. Beautiful kids. Trust me. You need to get a ring on her finger, mate."

I'm not going to disagree with any of this. She, my Polish *kaczuszka*, is not picking up everything from his thick English vernacular. Perhaps for the best, for some of it is rather more vulgar than anything I had in mind for tonight. But she's certainly getting the gist. She keeps her focus on her trembling fingers, and her little cigarette project. It's not easy to roll one standing up. I wonder what she's thinking.

And I smile, enjoying some of the images he's spinning. Though my insides are in knots. Make her mine? My future wife? These things, I want them too much to let them into my head. *This man is taking my thoughts too close to the sun.*

At last, she is done. He lights the roll-up she's just made, chattering away about our bright future and children, and warning us against the bottle, which he dangles before our eyes.

I sense it's time to remove ourselves. He's had us for several minutes, and we'll be here all night if he gets his way. He demands one last knuckle-touch from us both, and then we leave him to his wine, and his night, and his lost fatherhood.

I think of the suffering he must know, alone on the streets, probably having lost someone he loved. More than likely through inattention or self-destruction. It won't happen to me. I draw her closer with my arm.

But all those things he said…uncanny. The ramblings of a lunatic? A drunkard's nonsense? Sure. But was it *destiny* that we stumbled into a lunatic drunkard? One who'd been given the perfect script to read to a shy couple on a date? I want to believe it.

As we walk away, my chilly hand nestles in the warm folds of the black, soft hood at her nape.

~

I can feel the dream getting closer. My lips on hers. *My lips on hers!* Gentle. So gentle. Her lips on mine. *Her lips on mine!* It's coming. I've never felt stars align like this.

We've strolled some more, peering into the magnificent old college archways, beneath the glare of their surly porters. We passed her favourite sushi place. Took a short cut through a pub, where in winter she likes to come for the marshmallow roast, and down an alleyway. Finally, to the steps outside the Bodleian Library.

We're sitting down and looking at the Radcliffe Camera. It's round and it's grand and it's ancient, and we're close together, and she's beautiful, and everything is perfect. She's preparing her second roll-up of the night. My hand rests on her knee. It may be covered in thick denim, but I am still ravenous for that hint of a touch.

We joke about smoking. She's been at it since she was fourteen. I've never touched one. It's not the kind of high I want. Only someone like *her* can bring that. "I can't believe you've never been curious," she chides. "You really should try it once."

"I don't know if I should let you corrupt me that easily!" I argue. "It's quite a record you'd be wrecking. And you already tried to get me drunk tonight." I'm referring to the pint of cider we shared, of which she took only three sips. Yeah, I counted every drop of alcohol that went into her. It was precious little.

She titters her girly little laugh, and drops the subject for a moment. I'm learning that my black-loving, dress-hating raven still has feminine charms she can't hide. She's shivering with cold, though she stubbornly denies feeling the air's bite. She admits to getting distracted by shopping sometimes, though she's more likely to walk away with a panda-theme pencil box than trendy clothing.

She likes anything panda. *Why is this so impossibly cute?* I make a mental note for the first present I buy her. Which will be very, very soon, I tell myself. And as for the cold, I find myself pressing closer, wrapping my arm tight around this precious, fluffy bundle.

She finishes rolling her cigarette, and scratches in her pockets for her lighter. She doesn't do handbags. "Are you gonna try?" she questions.

"If I do, what's *your* challenge?" And I go for broke. On a whim. "I think you should give me a kiss."

She doesn't skip a beat. "Hmm, I will think about it!" *Yes!* She's not offended. Her tone drips with promise. That felt flirty. No doubt, now. She knows it's coming. I feel safer this way. And there's no hurry.

I let her smoke, and we share ghost stories while we watch Oxford's night owls scurry across the history-laden cobblestones. I am captivated and seduced by everything she says and thinks. My *kaczuszka*. I sit on her left and admire her pale, perfect hands, with their black-painted fingernails. Not a style I normally like. But this woman transcends style. She makes me forget those tastes I thought I had. And nothing can ruin the purity of her wonderful, soft face, white as snow.

Her lips on mine. My lips on hers. I shudder. It's going to happen. Tonight! Rarely is my life like a storybook, but my time has come.

I'm going to walk her home now. I feel our moment coming closer. As we rise from our perch on the cold stone steps, I fish beneath her baggy fur sleeves and find her right hand.

"Come on, fiancée," I joke. "I should really take your hand if we're to be engaged."

"It's a little early," she giggles. But she lets me take her tiny fingers in mine.

"Of course it is, *kaczuszka*, don't you worry," I smile back. "I'm not gonna be surprising you *just* yet."

And nor will I. What matters — *the only thing that matters in the world right now* — is that her soft, warm, pretty little hand is wrapped up in mine. The walk to her home is a long one. 30 minutes will pass. 30 golden minutes. The first 30 minutes holding her hand. I love that I feel confident enough to take it slow. I love that this feels so natural. So inevitable.

We pass the pub where she and her friends drink. I lock into her fingers a little tighter here, but she seems cool with this. I *won't* let her go. Further up Parks Road, she lets me smell her fingers. And yes, it's a pleasant aroma. Seductive naughtiness.

Closer to her home, deeper into the night, I rub the pad of my thumb across hers. The tiniest sensation of brushing skin, and I feel king of the world. I have done this! All by myself! With the clumsiest of lines at an exhibition!

I owe that drunken hobo a…well, maybe not a drink. I don't know, but something good. He sent us a vibe, and I've run with it. I can't stop smiling. Every breath is even sweeter than the last.

And now, we're at her house. I let go of her hand and we exchange pleasantries. It's good night kiss time. I've never been more ready. I've never been less concerned.

I lean in to embrace her, slipping my hands around her coat and cupping her shoulder blades. I ease my lips confidently towards hers.

And she turns her cheek.

I don't move, just raise my eyebrows. I look down at her as I hold her there, time standing still. She looks away to her right.

"You know I want that kiss…"

"Actually, I'm fine. Thanks."

What? *Who took her copy of the script?*

My brow furrows but I compose myself quickly, keeping hold of her. I'm more amused than anything. We've had such a fun-filled evening, I can't bring myself to get annoyed. It's all good. The hand-holding was enough to go on.

"What, because I didn't smoke your cigarette, huh?" I chuckle.

She mumbles something I don't recall, and disengages.

Yet still I feel okay. *Fine, she needs more time.* She's got some guy on the go — or at least she thinks she does. She feels guilty. Maybe confused. Or both. She'll kiss me next time. And it'll be all the sweeter for the wait.

"Give me a wave from your window, okay?" I say to her.

She nods as she turns and walks across the road. I watch her go, watch her unlock the door and go inside. I can see her silhouette going up the stars inside the mottled church-style window, and I see the light flick on in her second-floor room.

She comes straight to the curtain and waves cheerfully. I wave back, and blow her a kiss. She blows me one back. And I feel okay.

When I get home, I text her:

Thank you for a great night. You made it special just by being you. And just so you know, I will not be giving up on you! Good night, and nice dreams please.

She replies right away:

I had a great night too. Thank you too and good night.

There's a smiley at the end. And I do sleep well. I will leave her for a couple of days, then start planning the next date. The night I truly win her over. The night we have our magic first kiss.

The next day, all I can think of is *her*. When I get home from work, I decide to put my thoughts to good use, and write. About her. About our night. I have so much to say. So many vivid pictures to paint, though words can never suffice.

I'm a page and a half into this manuscript, buried in the joy of describing her. Absorbed in the pleasure of sharing her beauty, her radiance, the way she has lit up my life.

And halfway through the sentence you've already read — the one where the author got interrupted — her name flashes up on my phone. *Kaczuszka!* My little duckling! I pick up the handset and read what she has to say.

Hey, I wanted to say that it was very nice yesterday and thank you for that but I wanted to make clear that I see you only as a friend.

The f-word. A dagger to my heart. A blade sunk deep, and quickly, and twisted.

The word I loathe most. The one I cannot bear to hear from a beautiful woman I crave. Anything but *that* word.

That word, the one I deliberately tempted her to use long before I reached the point where it would crush me. And yet still she waited to use it. Waited until the moment I was committing her wonder to the written page. Until the moment she'd given me enough hope to dream. Given me enough of a taste to salivate.

And those misplaced letters, halfway through a sentence about Snow White? They stand as testament to a laptop hurled against the wall. To a flood of tears. To a phone launched against the same wall, propelled in blind, hyperventilating fury.

The f-word. Dagger to my heart. Dagger to my heart. Dagger to my heart.

~

Ravens. Unusually intelligent birds. Highly adaptable. Omnivorous and opportunistic. Collective noun: a conspiracy. Considered in many cultures as birds of ill omen or death.

~ Contemporary extract from a popular encyclopaedia ~

My brown eyes steal another furtive glance in the huge mirror. She's still impassive, her eyes firmly down. They're locked on her work. They give nothing away, and they don't meet mine for an instant.

I try to stop my own eyes from slipping down her reflection. But they will not be told. They rove to the velvety expanse of skin beneath her throat. And down, down to that taunting, nascent cleavage of hers. So slight and so subtle a hint. Yet it's enough. Like the sight of the poised front legs of a spider, waiting at its lair for passing prey. It's laced with potency. It's a sign of danger.

This is April. *My* April. And today…is my second haircut with her.

Two tiny dark patches, just where her chest begins to flower. Where that artful, gentle rise begins, infinitesimally, before the peeking line of her bra steals the show. Those little patches are my hair. They've fallen down on her while she's trimmed me. They've settled in perfect symmetry. I close my eyes, utterly defeated. By the thought that a part of me is nestling against her flesh and her heat…*there*.

April doesn't seem to have noticed. *Snip. Snip. Snip.*

Oh, but she is *beyond* beautiful. And I have nothing to do, in this chair, but marvel at her doll's face in the cruel, taunting mirror. Her deep brown eyes transfix me. They're round and big, and set wide apart. So wide apart that they don't look at you straight. Each one looks out to the world from its own side of her face, as if keeping a secret from the other.

The effect is bewitching. And it's impossible to look away from them. So big, they can't help but seem curious. So open, I should be able to read volumes of experience in those pools, inky in the middle and chestnut all around. Yet I see nothing. Nothing I can be sure of.

There's a dark tint of makeup around the edges of those eyes. It covers her soft eyelids too. Proud, confident black lashes frame the scene. That makes her expansive whites stand out like boiled eggs in onion soup. Everything else about her is so dark.

She tilts my head to one side. Ever so gently.

Ah yes, dark. Her brown hair, her tanned olive skin, her delicate little eyebrows, wide and high above those mysterious orbs. She is born and bred English, but she's almost dark enough to be a mix. It's not a Mediterranean kind of dark. Maybe a parent, or a grandparent, is black. Those *eyes*. There's something about them that makes me keep flying closer. I want to drown in them, like some wretched fly.

Snip. Snip. Snip. Not a frown, not a worry. Rarely a word. She's not one of those cheerful, chatty hairdressers. She gets on with it. *Oh April, could you know my thoughts?*

There is an acre of space in the triangle between her eyes and the subtle bridge of her nose. Less so beneath her bold, round nostrils, where her proud dimple meets an exaggerated cupid's bow. *Ah, cupid, where are you?* Her ripe young lips, just lightly touched with pinkish lipstick, are thin yet juicy, like artfully sliced strawberries.

Her neat, white upper teeth peep out now and then when she smiles. Which happens again now, as I tell her something about my week. It's probably not that amusing. Who cares? It's a cute little mouth, lips sealing seamlessly together. Zipped, but with a dimple either side. She's a dream for a doll modeller.

This is a boiling summer's day. The air-conditioning in the salon is labouring. She's got too many layers on. Not just the modest turquoise tank top and the black bra beneath: there's something like another tank top in between *those* layers.

That layer is brown like her eyes. Cut higher, more modest than the outer garment and bra, it's a cleavage stealer. I am relieved she's showing less than last time. It's good for my health. But I'm surprised that she needs this many clothes on such a day.

It's silent in here, most of the time. Our polite pleasantries have become intermittent. The online radio stream keeps cutting out. A couple of fifty-something ladies flick through magazines as some poor soul crafts their complex styles. I feel smug that I've got April.

I look at her pale, tight-fitting jeans. She is a picture today. It's a very trendy look. But her legs look skinny in those. Momentarily I am terrified, the memory of our conversation about the contents of her fridge — just cheese — screaming at me inside my brain. Is she anorexic? *God, please, no! I hate that.* I look at her bronze, shiny shoulders and smooth, bare arms. They are normal and fleshy. Not match sticks. I relax a little.

Her face: still expressionless. Can you see an eating disorder in someone's eyes? Can you see lust? I see neither. They are like black holes. How many have drowned in those, I wonder? *Snip. Snip. Snip.*

She moves around me now, near my left temple. She works her way across my head, leaning in towards my face each time she has to reach for the far side. *Touch me. Bend closer, April.* I look in the mirror. There is too much daylight between the mound of her torso and my shoulder.

No, wait, stay where you are! Suddenly there is touch. I am hardening beneath my cape, thinking of her naked, shorn of all that garb. I close my eyes, try to think of anything else. Oh, but that skin, it would be molten caramel, to taste and to see. Not a tan line in sight. I just know it.

I feel warm breath on me. Was it hers, a delicate airborne caress from her little low-bridged nose? Or was it another tepid gust of air from the door? I'm getting too dizzy to tell. It's the heat. *Her* heat.

Her elbow. It's under my nose. Her bent left arm is doing something to my hair with scissors. But my world, now, is just me and this flesh of hers. I am close enough to smell it. *Do. Not. Lick.* Oh, but look! She *does* feel heat. There is the most feminine, delicate trace of tacky perspiration on the crook of her arm. It makes morning dew look like a flood. I have to close my eyes. Or I *will* kiss April there.

On she goes with her trimming. *Snip. Snip. Snip.* Why do they always do that in threes? She is a haircutting machine, that's for sure. She won't be a trainee for long. Not with this kind of focus. Is she thinking anything at all? *A thousand Pounds for your thoughts.* She's only just graduated. At least ten years my junior. And I want to ravish her.

The radio is back on now. It pumps out chart-topping beats. The kinds of tunes that repeat and repeat, urging, pushing, spiralling you in directions you don't want to go. With their relentless thumping, these songs goad all the reason out of me. They will make me lose control.

Where exactly can I look without inflaming my passions? Perhaps the floor is safe, free from temptation. Alas! She wears open shoes, and her bare toes, nails painted jet black, keep homing into view. Okay, I *could* look away. But I can't. Of course I can't.

It's the only bit of skin I can see anywhere south of her bra line. How can she ignite me with so little? These toes are gorgeous. Cute. Neat. Clean. Ready to suck, right now. Looking at the floor is not helping.

Do I look up again, to her elaborate hair, pinned in some kind of complicated style I don't understand? I am drawn to the strands that frame her smooth, angular cheeks. I am envious at how they can brush lightly on her soft skin, cupping her face with a caress no heavier than a fly landing on her face. *I want to do that.*

Oh, sweet April. If only you knew how much I want you. Right now. *Please don't ask me to stand.*

"April, can you fit another gentleman in at five?" It's the shrill voice of one of her colleagues.

Does she *have* to word it like that?

April frowns for the first time. Then she nods. No trace of a smile. *Why isn't she on the same dirty page I am?*

I'm at my own mercy now, helpless. Those words have steered my thoughts in a u-turn. I was just about holding firm in trying to keep my wicked imagination at bay. Now I am fully erect beneath the cloak, as I think of her *fitting me in*. All of me. Sweet mouth first, pretty pussy second. And then agreeing to take another at five. *Well, I'm not sure about that last part, April, but I admire your willing.*

Snip. Snip. Snip. The music is beating itself up to a frenzy. Her hand is steady, but my mind races. *Thump. Thump. Thump.* The beats. My heart. My blood. Who knows? *April.*

Finally the snipping stops. She stands up straight, admires her handiwork in the mirror. She cocks her head to one side — I think she's pleased. Yes…a modest little smile lights up her face, and those upper teeth appear. *Don't do that!* And now she catches my eye, unafraid, hands on hips, scissors hooked on her index finger.

"How's that for you?" she says, in a brisk tone that suggests this is always just a formality for her. The smile goes away. Tragically short. She's all business again.

She's done a neat job. A little on the slow side, as usual. But I'm not complaining. The view was too perfect. *Oh, fuck, she wants me to talk.*

There's a huge lump in my throat, and my pulse has quickened in time with the music. I can feel perspiration on my forehead. *What am I, thirteen?*

"Oh yeah," I say, sounding far more together than I feel. Wanting so much more than a haircut. "You're a star, April."

You're so much more to me. I just can't say it. You're so young. I shudder. There's a pregnant pause. Lethargic heat. Building beats. Behind us, one of her shuffling colleagues, who looks ready to die of boredom, pushes a broom around the floor. I look at me, in my cape. I look at us. Then her. She's looking at me now, in the mirror.

"Would you like a shower?"

A *what?*

I'm startled, and she can see it. I'm stumped for words. Have I just dropped out of reality? Back into fantasyland?

She smiles, warm and full this time: "It's a new idea we're trying. You know, get all the hair off properly. It gets everywhere, doesn't it? And you look like you're heading back to the office, right?"

"I guess it does…and yes I am…" I say, my eyebrows raised in curiosity. And now I'm thinking about those locks of mine that landed on her upper chest. I steal a glance — they're still there. *Stand still, baby, while I flick those off...*

She takes this as a yes, and jerks her head towards the back of the shop.

"Come on then," she says, pulling the cape off from my neck and whipping it away.

I wish I could read something in her voice. But it's as closed a book as her eyes are. Is this normal? Showering? Seriously?

Hell, I've got to stand up now. My dirty thoughts are coming home to roost. All I can do is pretend to take a big, lazy stretch. I think about board meetings. Things I need to delegate. It's a monumental effort, but somehow I manage to soften a little, and re-arrange myself as I stand up. Her colleagues seem oblivious. One's on the till. The other keeps sweeping. The others are engrossed in their styling.

"This way, follow me," she says, turning on her pretty heel. She leads us to a door right in the furthest corner of the salon. We pass through it into a tiny kitchen. Just a sink, a microwave, a kettle and a few teacups. Nothing unusual there. Beyond that I can see an open door to a toilet, but to the left of this is another door. It's closed.

She opens this door and stands aside to let me in. I walk into what is actually a decent-sized shower room. There's a small, wooden bench with a clean, white towel and hand towel folded on it. And there's a stool, topped with coarse green plastic. There's also a hairdryer and a dressing table with a mirror,

But my eye goes straight to the clear Perspex doors on the shower. It's tastefully tiled, looks squeaky clean. It's one of those simple, minimalist ones: a large, high-mounted, powerful head and two taps. Big enough for two. And she's standing right next to me, just making me long. I sigh, louder than I mean to.

This shower setup is weird, in a hairdresser place. Novel, you might say. But why not? I *do* find all those shavings itchy and irritating. And besides, I could do with a cold one. April has got me far, far too excited for mid-afternoon. Work beckons, and I can't go back there like this.

I turn around to thank her for the suggestion before she goes.

"Aw, thanks April, this is an interesting..."

I freeze. *What's she doing?* Sure as hell not listening to me!She's closing the door. *And she's still on my side of it.* In. Here. With. Me. She flicks the latch. We're locked in.

My heartbeat goes completely nuts.

And so does April. She shoves me roughly against the wall. She's stronger than she looks when she takes you by surprise. *What the...?*

"OK mister," she hisses through her teeth. "I saw how you looked at me out there."

Events have turned on their head. That's all I know. Her doll's face looks stern, harsh. As always, her eyes look receptive, yet secretive. Now I've got adrenaline thrashing through me. Was I too leery? *Am I in some kind of trouble here?* Careful what you say now.

She looks mad.

"You can't *do* that," she urges, her eyes fixed on my chest, her grip on my elbows tightening. I can definitely feel her warm breath on my shirt front now.

"Do *what?*" I ask, trying to keep my tone neutral and my hands at my sides. OK, maybe I pissed her off. But it's not a crime to look at a pretty girl. Or is it? Maybe it's considered harassment these days. The world's gotten pretty fucked up. And she's young. She's never known a world that isn't fucked-up and litigious.

She looks up at me and meets my eyes again. Her voice drops to a whisper. "Look at me like that without fucking me...you jerk!"

I close my eyes, my head spinning with relief, disbelief and thankfulness. Seriously, this has got to be a dream. I can't find words.

And I don't need to. She's pressing hard up against me. I'm grateful for the wall, because I'm reeling in every sense. I'm shocked and I need to catch my breath, but I can't because she's stood up on her toes and she's kissing me. With feeling.

This can't be happening. *April!*

And yet! Right now, her tongue is darting every which way in my mouth, wrestling mine as it goes. She cannot seem to get as deep as she wants, but that doesn't stop her trying. Have I ever been kissed with such need? How long has she been wanting this? Our appointment...did it torture her like it tortured me? Right now, as she pulls my neck closer with her hands, it looks like it did.

I'm fully hard again, but this time I don't care. There's a locked door and a willing, comely, doll-faced vixen attacking me. This girl is not shy after all. I love it.

I need to gather myself. Poor April is at full stretch. I take her by the waist and shuffle her gently across the room so I can sit on the stool in front of the dresser. Reading my mind, she straddles my lap, wraps her forearms around my neck again. Oh, that forearm. *Yes!* Before her mouth assails me again, a thought takes me. I reach up for her left arm, the one I fought to restrain myself licking as she worked.

Is this the softest skin on a woman's body? That precious skin in the angle of the elbow must come close. I bring it to my lips, losing myself in the sensation of smoothness and delicacy. My tongue flicks out, and, yes, I can taste a tiny trace of salt on this hot day, mingled with whatever body wash she used this morning. I lap gently at that place, then nibble it ever so slightly. I can feel her whimper.

I let her reclaim her arm, and she wriggles her waist closer. If she didn't know I was hard before, she knows now. We're wearing way too much.

We kiss a little more, only now there's a hand roving under my shirt, making me tremble and gasp as it moves. I have a feeling this is going to be animal. I sense she needs a quickie. She's at work, after all. Is this a regular thing she does? What do her colleagues think she's doing? I decide I don't care. And as for animal…that is *fine* with me right now.

She can't get enough kissing. Me neither. Just when I think I can't get any more aroused, she pushes a little deeper, our tongues find more of the other, and she holds the back of my head a little tighter. I let her take charge, keeping my hands on her hips. Or we'll overbalance. I love the sounds she's making. The groans, the pants and the heavy breathing. April is so into this, and doesn't mind showing it. She's taking charge, taking what she wants. Which also happens to be what I crave. That's so fucking attractive.

I haven't even replied to her little jibe. But the time for flirty banter is long past. Yeah, she made me a little worried for a moment back there, but things are turning out just fine. I'm all the more turned on for the contrast. Though she deserves a spanking for scaring me like that. *Next time, April.*

For now, I'm enjoying letting her have her way with me, the saucy little fox. Oh, what a thrill to see revealed the passion that was hidden behind those dark eyes! All along! I knew there were volumes in there!

Abruptly she hops off me and stands in front of me. And yes, my hair is still there on her, though one tuft has fallen right down to her bra line. "Are you going to give it to me then?" she says, hands on hips, eyeing the bulge in my jeans.

"Yes April," I reply, slowly, my eyes meeting hers as I slowly raise them. My confidence is back in residence. "I am going to give it to you. I will do as you ask."

"Good. Then I'll get naked for you," she says, raising one eyebrow naughtily. The word 'naked' sends me ballistic with impatient want. It always does. But I sit and wait.

She pulls the turquoise top over her head. Then the brown one. Now she's only in her black bra, but she doesn't hang around. This is a girl on a mission. She reaches behind her with one hand, flicks the clasp, and her delicious breasts spring free.

I sway at the sight of them. She looks down at them for a moment, frowns at the bits of my hair, the ones that had me fixating. She brushes them away with the side of her hand.

I tighten further as she does it, her left breast wobbling a little from the flick of her hand. It doesn't oscillate much though. Just enough to excite me. These are young, ripe, firm and precious. Her fresh, taut nipples are a dark brown. Of course they are. They match her eyes.

I'm stunned at the sight of her. Literally gasping. *Cherish moments like this. Give your mind, your soul, your everything to this. Yeah, fixate! Let her pull you in. Feel it! Live it. Every touch, every breath, every flash of her dark pupils: bottle them.*

I'm terrified I am about to wake up, this dream snatched from before my eyes. I cannot believe we are here, now, like this, holed up in the bathroom while at least two middle-aged ladies are having their perms done outside. *How did this happen?* I wanted her more than anything I've ever wanted anything. And here she is – I have her.

I reach out and grasp her by the waist, as if to satisfy myself that she's really there. Flesh and blood. *Purest April.* And I have to hold her, so that she can never melt away. My belief needs this touch. She pauses a moment as I jam my fingers under the tight belt of her jeans, enthusing in her body heat, and I gently run my thumbs across marshmallow skin just below her rib cage.

She indulges herself a moment, and I know it's doing something to her. And then she remembers where she is.

"Quickly, mister. They think I'm making a fucking cup of tea you know!"

I nod. No boss of hers is going to get between me and my April right now. In fact, even if this building went up in flames, I'd stay right here with her. As it is, I feel fire in my belly and see flames of lust dancing in her dark eyes. We may have to call the fire brigade anyway.

I don't want to take my hands away from her, though I know I need to escape my clothes. There's still this lingering fear that she'll disappear. She seems to sense this, and deftly unpicks the buttons of her jeans with her fingers. Her belt slackens, and my instincts take over.

I slide my palms down the outside of her thighs, my forearms dragging her denim down with them. I sink to my knees, eye level with her minuscule sky-blue panties, and keep pulling them down. When my hands reach her ankles, she lifts her cute feet out one at a time. The first wave of her feminine scent hits me, and I swoon. I am mesmerised again.

This would take all day if it were left up to me. It can't. "Pull down my panties," she whispers through her teeth, all urgency and need. Ah yes. Panties.

I could break these with one finger, so I'm gentle as I can be. I grab the string holding up the flimsy triangle covering her mound, and peel it down her legs. A strand of her wetness clings to that place at her core, reluctant to leave her, and dangles like a string of broken spider's web. She steps out of her underwear, and I have broken that web of hers.

April is naked. It tears me up that I only have her for a couple of minutes now. Kneeling before her, it takes everything I've got not to put my tongue there, right in that moist, gushing brook between her legs. But I know that if I start, I will have to finish. And we don't have time.

She tugs gently on my chin, pulling me up to my feet. "OK, quickly now…keep your shirt on." Her fingers are already working at the buttons on my jeans. I love that she is unafraid to ask for what she wants from a man. It drives me wild when a woman seeks pleasure like that.

There's no ceremony as she yanks my jeans and my boxers over my uncomfortable bulge and down. When they get as far as my knees she loses interest and grabs my hips. "Back on the stool, mister. You've got everything I need there," she says, eyeing what's just sprung free from my trousers.

I do as she asks. I think she's going to ride me. I push the stool closer to the dresser, so I can support her better. *Fuck, this is exciting.*

April is on a mission. Before I even know it, she's astride me, standing on the tips of her toes. She takes my erection in her fingers and guides it between her legs. And she looks right into my eyes as I enter her. Although it feels like she's entering me. *Oh yes, that's it, baby.* She's looking right into my soul as she slips seamlessly onto me. I fill her completely. She is *fitting me in* at last. And she is so wet.

She wants to get going. And she doesn't need my help. She's going to do this. Now that's she's sunk onto my length, her feet are comfortably on the floor. She slips her arms beneath my shoulders and curls her hands up beyond them to grip the back of my neck. It feels sensational already.

Now April begins to ride. I was right — this is animal. I have to brace myself, holding my elbows on the dresser as she thrusts. But I'll do anything I have to, to keep on having what I've got now. Her soft throat is just in front of my face, her head thrown back as she slams on and off me, powered by her determined little legs.

My eyes feast on the scene as she lets herself go, burying herself in and out of my lap. For her they are hammer blows, but for me it's just pleasure. A delicate woodland fairy having her way with me.

I can feel the pace, the urgency, the mighty effort she's putting in, but she's so soft and tiny that she won't hurt me. All I need to think about is keeping our stool steady, and the wonderful thing that's happening to me.

She's breathing hard, lost in what she's doing. Her eyes are closed now. I know she's building and it's an effort for her to keep silent, but she has to. Her energy is terrific, and she's pressing closer to me now, keeping the delicate balancing act going as her bouncing breasts slap and slam — gently as a woodland creature! — into my willing forehead. *I want this always, April.*

This closeness has me going now, and I feel myself reach the point of no return. She's gulping huge, silent gasps, now, her thrusts no softer, but I sense she's at that place too. Controlling everything as she is, turned-on as she was, it hasn't taken long. Building, building...

I can't resist a tiny whisper. "I'm coming, baby, I'm coming..." She responds with a noise from somewhere deep in the back of her throat, savage yet almost imperceptible. The sound tells me she's desperate to scream out loud, but this is the best she can do.

Hearing this suppressed groan of unbridled lust is the last straw for me. I tighten, twitch, unleash into April. I dance inside her and she clenches around me, pulling hard on my hair and digging her elbows hard into my armpits, uttering that otherworldly screaming whimper again.

And now she slows, not moving her upper body from that clasping lock she's got me in. Her hips are gyrating gently now, doing a couple of victory laps as they slow down. She buries her chin on top of my head, as if she wants to cling to me all day and all night.

I know she can't do that. I want that too. I feel physically ill at the thought that she will have to pull off me now. She seems to have lost her will. She's still somewhere up in the clouds. Something inside me makes me sense I have to take the reins now, if just for a moment. So, flying in the face of everything I want right now, I whisper to her again. "April... you gotta go."

I want to slap myself for saying it, but I've done the right thing. She relaxes her lock just a little as my words sink in. Even that tiny hint of uncoupling is awful. Closing my eyes at the dreadful thing I have to do,

I unsheath her tiny body from my lap, lifting her up and placing her on her shaken, overworked legs. She smiles, sniffs and wipes her nose.

"You look perfect, don't worry," I reassure her. "Get dressed and get back out there."

I want to slap myself again. April nods, her wits coming back to her. "You should still have that shower," she says, jerking her head at the cubicle as she picks up her panties from the floor. I nod back, but first I want to watch her get dressed. I want to savour every last moment of her nakedness. I can take my time.

She smiles, looking completely relaxed again, as she puts her panties back on. I feel my spirits drop as my pure, nude April slowly starts to disappear like a beach beneath a rising tide. But she never takes her eyes off mine as she tugs her jeans on, does up her bra and quickly pulls her tops back over her body, and that makes me feel better. April's eyes are a feast on their own.

She's dressed. *Ugh.* She's going. *Ugh!* I want to sink. She skips quickly to the shower and turns on the taps, taking a moment to adjust them to a comfortable temperature as she holds her hand beneath the stream. Then she steps across to me, pulls my head down towards hers and places a soft kiss on my lips. It crushes me.

A final smile, a quick check for the all-clear outside the door, and she slips out. I undress completely and shower, my brain feeling like fudge. *Did that really just happen?* It seems so outlandish that I don't have the capacity to soak up the last waves of pleasure.

I stare at the closed door and wonder if anyone noticed she'd gone for a while. What an incredibly daring young woman. I *love* that she did that. I *love* that she let her lust overcome her and cornered me in here. And if she's done it before, then good for her. *April gets what April wants.*

I'm so turned on by her taking me that even now, towelling myself down, my erection is only just starting to fade. I'd almost forgotten this is exactly what I wanted too. I smile to myself once more. It might be awkward out there. Yeah, I might be best off finding another hair-dresser. But boy, April...you made my day today. And to me you'll always be the finest hairdresser in the world.

PLAYDATE

For the first time in three years, I was single. The break-up was painful, but it had to be done. It played out over Skype, because I'd just taken on a three-month assignment on the other side of the world. Australia. I had thought about the split for weeks, and now it couldn't wait any longer.

My suggestions of a six-month break, or an open relationship, were rejected. So we were through. That warm Sunday afternoon was a tearful one. It doesn't get much worse than a Skype break-up that doesn't involve a fight. You can't do a hug, and that makes you well up inside.

My crazy hippie Aussie room-mate's response had been typically Antipodean. She handed me a beer, her car keys, and told me to take a drive.

I survived. And when my eyes had dried, I began the cheering-up process. I was, after all, in the Great Southern Land. And from what I'd read, Australia was the randiest country on earth.

Perth, state capital of vast Western Australia, was a million miles from anywhere. I didn't know a soul within four hours (by plane!) of its friendly, sun-drenched metropolis. I was free to play and needed a boost. If ever there was a time to give hookup websites a try, this surely had to be it.

A quick web search led me to Australia's favourite one-stop sex site, *Red Hot Pie*. Dot com. Dot Au. A no-strings-attached online 'dating' facility. It was exactly what I was looking for. And a cursory glance suggested there was plenty of activity.

Then, a little more nosing around Google told me that *Red Hot Pie* had once been caught using fake profiles. But that embarrassing business had been a couple of years earlier. And now that they'd been rumbled, surely they were squeaky clean? Surely everyone user on there was legit? Now that I thought about it, the fact they'd been caught made them the logical choice for an experiment, didn't it?

I decided I could afford $20 for a month's worth of finding out. Second chances and all that. I knew I would have to put in some time. A month of solid effort that would perhaps, God willing, reward me with my deepest fantasy. An erotic, lust-driven dream that my now-mourning girlfriend had been unprepared to share with me.

I had certainly wanted her to be a part of my most intimate desires, and, God knows, I tried to twist her arm enough times. But in the end, she just could not make peace with the concept. Even though my needs were so close to things she'd done in the carefree youth that she now insisted on consigning to history.

Agreeing to go to my deathbed without experiencing *that* thrill? Too much to ask. A thrill my ex had openly fantasised about herself, especially in our early months, but which she became increasingly adamant she would always deny me.

It had never crossed my mind to cheat on her, of course, though I'd had my chances. There were far bigger reasons for our break-up, but this impasse was one little thing that helped it along. I simply couldn't make peace with the idea of *not* acting out a fantasy we both had in our minds.

But now I *could* act it out. I could do what I wanted.

And so I excitedly filled out my profile on *Red Hot Pie*. I wasn't brave enough to put a photo of my face online. Just me in a towel, from the neck down. Faces could always be sent to individuals, or uploaded to a private folder. One had to be careful, after all, especially when one had a professional work life to maintain.

Professional work life was a million miles from my thoughts as I checked the boxes. Wow, they'd thought of everything! Did I like giving anal? (Was the Pope Catholic?) Did I like *receiving* anal? (No way, Jose!) Did I like giving oral sex? (Put your pussy on a plate and let me dine...) Did I like receiving oral sex? (Seriously, did they even *need* that box?) Naturism? (Smiley face!)

The wonderfully depraved list went on. My fantasy was on there too, of course. Plus some things I'd never heard of. I had to look up what *bukkake* was, for instance. A Japanese word referring to something the country's porn producers invented as a way around its censorship laws. It was where several guys ejaculated on a girl's face.

Now then, what age was I looking for? I pushed the upper limit close to fifty. I knew all too well how much fun a cougar could be. Zero inhibition was the main thing for me. And experience always showed in the bedroom. Plus my chances were better than with a 22-year-old. Girls in their twenties were fussy, whimsical and didn't know what they wanted.

Then I started messaging. I knew it wouldn't be easy. I'd heard that girls on sites like this — or even regular dating sites — could get dozens of messages a day. Standing out would be hard. One thing I'd read was that *not* sending a picture of your equipment would be a good way to do so.

So, even on a sex-fuelled site like this, I had to come up with some words that were witty or eye-catching! It was the tiresome reality of the world again: women owned sex, and there was never any shortage of demand. I had to market myself.

I did my best to write charming, cheeky words. And I did not send out any penis photos. I tried always to respect them as people, which wasn't difficult. That part came naturally enough. Especially if the woman was liberated, grown-up and open-minded enough to be on a site like this.

After a few days, though, I began to get despondent. Had I wasted my time and money on this deafening silence? Were these people fakes after all? Thinking about it, there did seem to be an endless supply of profiles for a relatively small city. Or were these ladies just ignoring me? Which was it?

A couple of women favourited me, but even these proved impossible to talk to. Messages went unanswered, no matter how polite. Maybe they had fifty guys chatting them up. My check-ins to *Red Hot Pie* were looking increasingly hopeless.

So I tried a change in strategy. New thinking that would change my outlook for good.

Instead of choosing to contact the women with hottest pictures, I went for ones who didn't have photos at all. I reasoned that these profiles would surely be real — why would *Red Hot Pie* make a fake profile if not to draw you in with a comely blonde vixen?

There'd surely be fewer guys bombarding a girl with no photo. And, now that I thought about it, an empty photo frame didn't necessarily mean she was ugly. She could just be private and shy, like me. Or she could be a first-timer. Also like me. She might be my perfect match!

Maybe she was the sexiest of the lot, but just wanted you to focus on the words in her profile. And soon enough, I found some words I liked very much.

PinkAngelCake. Cute username! Age: 39. Orientation: Bisexual. So far, so good. She'd ticked nearly every box. Receiving anal sex? Tick. Giving oral sex? Tick. Naturism? Tick. She'd even ticked *bukkake.* Something tightened in my pants as I read her most intimate desires, even distilled as they were to simple check-boxes. *Even without a photo.*

This woman sounded like a lot of fun. I was already getting the curious feeling that looks were not going to be much of a factor. I read her short profile with interest.

'I am a recently separated mother. I'm definitely not looking for a relation-ship, but I have a weakness for younger men. I can be incredibly naughty, and I love to give as well as to receive in the bedroom.'

That's when I realised how sexy frankness was. I loved how she got straight to her point. The very simplicity of her words made them sizzling hot! This cupcake lady, she sounded on my wavelength. She was going to get a message.

So I wrote to her, portrait included. My note was brief and to the point. I could see that she wasn't a paid-up member, so she wouldn't be able to reply anyway. All I could do was give her my number, and hope for the best.

That very same night, my phone vibrated. One shot, one hit! Breakthrough!

Hey, it's PinkAngelCake. I liked your profile, let's talk. My name's Carly. Xx

I sucked in the cool winter air through pursed lips. Oh God, I had my first message. A *sex site* message. Her tone…well, she sounded just as fun as her profile had made her sound. *Carly.* Excitement began to coil in me, and still I hadn't given a thought to how she might look.

Right away, this Carly was open. At that very moment, she was apparently at a friend's house, in a mixed crowd, 'fooling around dressing and undressing each other'. I wasn't sure exactly what that meant, but it didn't sound bad at all.

I asked her for a photo right away. I didn't think she wanted to mess around. And she didn't: a few minutes later an image came through to my crappy old Nokia. Pixelated and grainy, but I could see she was smiling into the camera, leaning in such a way that I could appreciate some ample cleavage peeping out from her tight black dress.

Her hair looked chestnut brown, neck length but untidy. As far as I could tell, she didn't have picture-perfect skin. She was patchily freckled, and, to be honest, she looked plain. And perhaps she wasn't the slimmest, either.

And yet…it didn't matter. My heat was rising. My excitement had taken me by the throat. There was something about the way she talked that was driving me wild already. A mix of her flirty manner and the fact that I knew she *wanted sex*. Her repetition of a need for younger guys. Plain? Who cared? She was doing things to me with her lust alone.

I beat out a quick reply.

Ooh, I think I'd like to be a fly on the wall over there! Although actually, if I were a fly, I'd probably be trying to crawl down that cleavage...xx

She took no offence. Within hours, we had arranged to meet. She lived a fair drive away, down the coast in Mandurah, but she agreed to come to the city.

Okay, I'll park at the station, take the train in, and meet you in Northbridge. Let's have a couple of drinks and see where the night takes us...xx

It was loaded with promise, that text. Yet even after how we'd met and the boxes we'd ticked online, it still seemed presumptuous for either of us to plan sex practicalities outright. Even on *Red Hot Pie*, it seemed you had to play the dating game a little.

But it would be wrong not to think of practicalities. We both knew where this was heading, even if we didn't say it out loud. My place was a no-no, as I had housemates. I didn't need an audience. If I went back to hers, well, I'd be in for a heck of a long train ride. If the worst came to it, there were always hotels.

We'd figure something out.

~

I found her sitting on the steps, right on time. Good girl! She wore a bright blue one-piece dress. Not showing off quite the cleavage I saw on that photo. It was fairly conservative, truth be told. And yes, she *was* plain. But so what? I was excited! I grinned at her, and she smiled back.

"I watched you go up and down the stairs a couple of times, looking kinda lost!" she chuckled after I give her a peck on her freckled cheek. "I knew it had to be you!"

"Aah, you caught me...I'm pretty bad at spotting faces," I confessed, "but since you were the only girl sitting on her own, waiting for someone..."

Waiting for *someone*? Waiting for *sex*. Fuck...that was a delicious thought. But I didn't say it out loud.

We decamped to the bar at the bottom of the steps, and each of us started gulping a cider. She was a little more nervous than I expected her to be, but I felt quite okay. Even though this was one almighty weird, new thing. I'd certainly never had a relationship like this before. One that started with sex talk and worked backwards towards a date. Now that we were face to face, small talk felt somehow contrived.

At first it was hard to get much out of her. Conversation didn't quite flow. But the first chance I got to seize upon a sexy innuendo — I forget what it was — she laughed and relaxed.

One naughty double entendre, and suddenly we'd both hit upon our wavelength.

Soon we were giggling and snickering about everything under the sun, and she was unleashed. We were not even through the first drink when she asked me what attracted me to her profile. I wasn't brave enough to mention her anal desires just yet, but told her I liked the things on her checklist.

"Especially that you said you were...into girls," I continued, broaching the subject that gripped me so. "And that you ticked the MFF box. That's...you know...one of my ambitions."

This was a key junction in my grand plan. *Shit, please don't run away now.* I held my breath.

But instead her face broke out in a mix of cheekiness and concern. She said, "What, hold on...you mean...you've never had a threesome?"

I shook my head with a wry smile, and flashed my eyebrows at her. We were cutting right to the chase tonight! The sun had barely set, and we were getting to the crux of things already. That fantasy I wanted so much to make reality.

"Oh, you poor boy!" she cooed. "I can't believe it! And you're so handsome too! Clearly you've been hanging around with the wrong girls."

I liked her choice of words. Her attitude made me want to take her down an alley right there and then. "I guess so," I said, looking her in the eye. "So then, how many have you had?"

"Quite a few, but when I was younger," she said. "Then I got married...had three kids...honestly, I just didn't even have sex for several years. You wouldn't believe it, but every night I stayed up watching crap television just to avoid going to bed with my husband."

I gawped at her. This experimental sex kitten was coming off a gigantic drought?

"It's only in the last couple of months, since I was brave enough to split from him, that I've started experimenting with fun again..."

My mouth went dry as I saw her saucy eyes twinkling at me, before she giggled into her cider glass once more. *Oh my...what a woman.* Her sexy talk made my desire go skyrocketing. My timing was looking pretty good here.

We moved to dinner at a sidewalk Italian. By then red wine was the drink of choice. She had just a small pasta starter while I ticked another little box I wanted to tick: eating *arancini*. Even though my appetite had almost gone, and I couldn't finish the delicious risotto balls. My hunger was for other things now.

It was clear which way the evening was going. Our talk had become free and frank. She revealed that her friend Liz was in a hotel just around the corner, *that very night*, with her husband. Liz was more than a friend, actually. They'd played together of late. Liz's husband had played too.

By that stage we were openly talking about having our way with each other that night, and where exactly that was going to happen. Out loud, she toyed with the idea of calling Liz to see if we might all have some fun in that hotel room.

I almost choked on my *arancini*. This was moving faster than I could have dared dream. Perhaps too far, even. I liked the hotel room and I liked the idea of Liz. But there had never been another guy in my fantasies.

"Liz knows I'm out on the town with you tonight," she grinned as she took out her phone. "She's pretty excited about the possibilities."

So was I. And it showed. Standing up any time soon would be an impossibility. My jeans were far too tight for that. *Was this woman for real?*

Texts flew back and forth. Finally Carly decided against the idea. It seemed Liz's husband was in a bit of a mood tonight. I was almost relieved.

"So, it's back to just us, then?" I grinned. Group sex could always wait for the perfect moment.

"Yeah, but where?" she said with a wolfish smile. "Do you like doing it in public...outside?"

"Sure, I'm not against that," I smiled back at her. "But don't you think a place of our own would be more relaxing for a first...you know!"

"It would," she agreed. "But my place is *miles* away and you're telling me yours is out of the question..."

"Well, it's either a bush in King's Park, or we go *miles*. Bush is last resort for me. I'd rather we have somewhere to enjoy ourselves properly. I'm off work tomorrow you know. I really don't mind..."

I waited with bated breath. I'd have gone to the end of the earth for her that night. All I wanted was her and a bedroom. But I knew she was worried about kids and exes floating around her place.

"Well, I do have an empty house until lunchtime," she mused. "But I've been drinking! I can't drive us home from the station, can I? We'd need a taxi, then you'd need another one in the morning, and...argh! You know, I was rather hoping we'd just be going to your place, you silly man!"

I gulped, praying that practicalities weren't going to overcome the burning lust going on right now. I couldn't, simply *couldn't*, do my place. And in the spirit of openness, I told her why.

"Yeah, maybe I would, but something unexpected happened last night. It's...you see...I slept with my housemate."

I closed my eyes, fearing her reaction. Was this to be the dumbest confession of all time? I'd only volunteered this information because this woman seemed beautifully liberated. She was, after all, registered on a no-strings attached hookup site. Still, you never knew where jealousy would well up in a girl. That honesty Tourette's of mine needed fixing.

But she merely laughed. "I see! Root rat, you are!" I got the gist of her

Aussie slang. "Okay, I understand. You can't do that to her. You're right…your house is definitely out!"

I wondered for the umpteenth time if Carly could possibly be for real. She was utterly unfazed that I'd slept with another woman the night before. Technically the same day, now that I thought about it. And she was cool with it.

Her willing only increased my current lust levels. I coughed. "Look, I'm a guy, my alcohol threshold is higher. And I've only had a couple of glasses. I can switch to coke now…if you'll let me drive your car from the station…we could make this work?"

She thought about it for a second, then beamed at me. "Well, if you don't mind squeezing into my weird little wagon…! Okay, how about we go somewhere for one more drink, then catch the last train?"

I squeezed her hand and we paid the bill. We split it down the middle, laughing at how different this was from a regular date. Nobody was pretending to make a life partnership here — she had been actively clear on that — and we'd already planned our fun at home. So who needed to play old-school dating games with the dinner payment?

Not us. And I liked it. Why couldn't all of life be this honest?

Carly is *incorrigible* on the train heading south out of Perth Central. We're forced to stand, as other revellers have snatched all the seats on this last service away from town. She keeps pressing against me, hooking her fingers into my belt, murmuring about how she can't possibly wait to get home.

She looks up at me, biting her top lip lasciviously. Time and again I have to remind her that she's going to embarrass me. I can't hide excitement like she can — not that she's making much effort herself — and I am feeling a terrific build-up in my jeans.

Again I wish that some company would invent the opposite of Viagra for guys like me. It feels like people are looking. They certainly can't be in any doubt that I've got a fantastically frisky lady for company. They'd have to be blind to miss it. "Stop it!" I hiss at her. "Just hang in there!"

She keeps burying her horny little head in my chest, groaning with frustration and pent-up lust. It does nothing for the bulge beneath my buttons. I make it clear that fooling around under a bush in a dark park is one thing, but a busy commuter train is quite another. We're *not* doing it here. She giggles, and says she never would, really. I'm not convinced.

She's still a little breathless after our dash to make sure we caught the train. She had to remove her heels and run barefoot. "I'm gonna need a wash, when we get home, you *do* know that?" she says. I nod, hoping she won't take that line of conversation any further just yet. I am desperate to think clean thoughts right now.

I'm thankful when two seats free up, and we grab them. I have to hobble along the carriage, close behind her, wishing I could make my crotch invisible. Maybe nobody's remotely interested enough to have noticed. Maybe they're all just being polite. Either way, I'll be glad when I get this excitable bundle of hormones home.

It's an hour before we pull into Mandurah, the last stop on the coastal line. The longest hour of my life. She yanks me off the train by the hand.

Before I know it, I'm hunched up in the driver's seat of her car, which is like something out of a cartoon. It's a bit…special. The roof's too low and every control is somewhere unusual. The handbrake is on the dash, and the indicators are buttons. From where I'm sitting, the thing looks like it's been made up of spare parts from the scrapyard.

But it'll get us back to her place, and that's all that matters.

I follow Carly's directions, out of the station and onto the broad streets of a town that's brand-new to me. I'm driving a brand-new car, with a brand-new woman. At one in the morning. If nothing else, *Red Hot Pie* is taking me on the most extraordinary adventure. And the best is yet to come. Though it's not a story I'll be able to share with many.

She giggles every time I fumble with the bamboozling semi-automatic gearshift, but bites her lip again when I place a hand on her thigh.

"Nearly there!" she announces. *Thank God.* She's got *her* hand on *my* thigh now. And she's sighing heavily, filling the car with her warm long-ing. "Take a left here. Then you go right...and...here! It's the house on the corner!"

I pull up, but can't figure out how to turn the engine off. This car seems to have a lot of extra switches that other vehicles can do without. She laughs at me. "Yeah, I know...I hate this stupid car too! Let me do it." She leans across me, her ample breasts pressing shamelessly against my shoulder, and finally silences the motor.

Then she looks across at me and gives me the most wolfish of grins. "Shall we go inside?"

"Hell yes!" is all I need to say. We trot quickly up the path to the front door. She is *so* excited, and that's the biggest turn-on I can remember in years. Last night included. My housemate is ten out of ten hot, and still in her twenties, but did she give me this kind of enthusi-asm? No, she just lay there with her legs open. No wonder I need some-thing more tonight!

Carly failed to lock the door behind her when we came in, but I made sure I did it. And double-checked. What I had in mind did not call for surprise visitors. Especially ex-husbands or kids. I didn't understand why she was so careless. Though if it was passion that made her do it, then it was kinda hot.

The preamble and the bullshit and the long journey were over. She muttered something about drinks, but neither of us really wanted to play that game. I raised no objection when, ten seconds after we'd passed through the door, she invited me to follow her to the shower.

"You want to clean up together?" she asked. A completely unneces-sary question. One that launched a sexual whirlwind so violent that piecing any of it together is like trying to reassemble prehistory. She was not in a mood to stand on ceremony this evening. She stripped without a care, and I stripped without a hesitation.

She stepped into the shower. I joined her.

She grabbed the shower head and began to spray her body down with warming water.

I grabbed the hose from her when she was done. Though I was still feeling pretty clean, I gave my raging erection a few purifying splashes. Before I was even halfway done, she was down on her knees and had me in her mouth. And sucking with obvious enjoyment.

We'd been in the door, what, two minutes? Our clothes were scattered all over the floor. The bathroom door was wide open and water was flying everywhere. She couldn't see it, but I shook my head at the scene. She'd brought me, a stranger from the internet, back to her house, and was brazenly fellating me in her shower. Milking me and loving it.

Some would insist on calling her names, for being a woman who would delight herself doing things like this with a man she'd just met. Well, fuck those prudes. They were the losers, because with each moment, Carly was growing more beautiful before my very eyes.

Her base, animal desire had totally won me over. It had the power to transcend the superficial. I *loved* her need. I *loved* her groans. I didn't *care* how she looked. Just the way her head was bobbing, the way her mouth and tongue was slurping, were all the turn-on I could ever want.

She was teaching me things tonight. I was learning how much I wanted a woman who *wants* it. Who really, *really* wants it. A woman who begs for what she needs, then demands it, then takes it. A woman who screams out her wishes and craves service. Yes *please*! Was this what I'd been missing in my years with passive partners? God!

We stumbled across the hallway, into her bedroom. She told me she liked rough sex. So I fucked her with such intensity that our condom broke.

Then she told me she liked her hair pulled, so I fucked her again, doggy-style this time, yanking on fistfuls of her crazed, damp-with-sweat mop, so that she yelped and growled and moaned and bucked, and came with a howl.

A few minutes biting her nipples *hard*, a few minutes with her head between my legs, and we were both ready to go again. She wanted everything that Thursday night. She skipped across to the top shelf of her cupboard, pulled out a box full of toys. And lube.

Moments later I slipped my length into her butt. It went easily. She lay flat on her stomach, elbows out and breasts squashed against the sheets. I rode on top of her back as I probed into her. A sensational feeling.

And still she demanded it rougher. "Fuck my tight little asshole!! Fuck it harder!! Yea…mmm…yeeaaah!! MMM!! FUCK my tight ass, go on, FUCK it!! Hard!! Mmm…*mmm*…oh God, oh my *God*!! Mmm…MMMPH!!

She buried her face in her pillow as she came again with my erection splitting her, shattering the room with her heaving orgasm, just moments before I came again, unleashing inside her most secret cranny.

And there we lay, naked and panting, drenched in sweat. But merely for moments. Still she wanted more.

We began to take it slower then. I ducked across the hall and washed myself. She waited for me on the wide, wonderful bed, its linen a crumpled mess now, her legs wide open. Even then, we'd barely kissed, and I was suddenly startled to remember that I didn't find myself drawn to her per the traditional laws of attraction. It had slipped my mind in all the fun.

I simply wanted to bury myself inside Carly, time and again. And it was all down to her spirit. What she lacked in looks, she surpassed in confidence and, more than that, *hunger*. It was so fucking attractive, that guiltless yearning of hers. The way she begged me to ride her so hard. She showed the finger to repression, and I loved it.

Oh, if only all the world's women were as uninhibited as this…well, the makeup firms would go out of business! So would *Cosmo*! Everything would be wonderful, and nobody would sleep alone for long. If only!

I loved that she wanted me and told me so and begged for what she wanted and made a noise when she got it. I loved that I didn't have to fawn and fawn and fawn, never knowing where I stood. I loved that I didn't have to play games. I loved that she showed all of her enjoyment to me. I wanted to come back for more already.

Next we found ourselves in a modified 69. I was on top, but also partly on my side. Her legs were still thrown apart, and I supped the delicious juices of her core, with big, long, lazy licks. Without warning she pulled my cheeks apart and began to tongue my ass. *Oh, yes!*

I'd only felt that once before, and that had been a tentative, duty-bound effort from my last girlfriend, who never did it again. Now I knew how good it could be. I could feel the *hunger* again from Carly's tongue. She *wanted* to be in there. She probed as far as she could go, unabashedly, all energy, all wanton lust to explore a man's every corner.

"You're gonna make me come again!" I gasped in between licks of her vagina.

"Well then, do it on my face!" she replied excitedly, twisting her head out from between my legs. "I fucking *love* it! I might pretend I don't though…"

In an instant I was kneeling above her, her shoulders locked loosely between my knees and her face poised beneath my erection. She closed her eyes as I started to rub myself, unconvincingly shaking her head and murmuring "no…*no*…"

Her hand gave her away, though, as she started to pull on her own hair even as she pretended to turn her face away. I played along and grabbed her chin straight while I quickened my own pace. "You keep *still* now," I hissed, as menacingly as I could manage. "I'm gonna come on your face. Do you hear me? Don't you *dare* keep moving."

She obeyed and whimpered. Her lips fell open. And I let go. Her face was drenched.

Plain? I had never seen anything so beautiful as her cream-spattered face. It was a picture of submission, liberation and guiltlessness. It was a picture of everything life could be if you allowed it to. It was a picture of a sexually sated woman, sated by me. And *nothing* could turn me on more.

Six days later, the weather was foul, grey and windy. Even Perth, the city that boasts more sunshine than any other on earth, could get like this in the depths of winter. But I certainly didn't care about that as I watched the water lash against the train window.

I was on the line to Mandurah once again. Destination Carly. And Liz. I was *en route* to my first threesome. The rain would only make it cosier.

It seemed odd to be doing this at nine o'clock on a Wednesday morning. But none of us were nine-to-five workers, and the girls both had kids, so nine o'clock it was. My first meeting with Carly had at least involved the pretence of a drink. This time, we were straight down to business. It was there in black and white, planned by text message.

I showed Liz your photo and she thinks you're handsome. She wants to play with us. She sucks cock very well! Are you free on Wednesday morning?

Was I free? I'd have cancelled tea with the queen! The text banter had started up again on the train ride, and I was thoroughly aroused by the time I arrived in Mandurah. Thankfully this was an empty train, as respectable morning commuters were all heading in the opposite direction.

I was most certainly *not* envious of anyone heading for a desk and computer screen this morning. I was heading for pre-arranged group sex. I licked my lips and shook my head. I couldn't imagine this was going to happen too often. In fact, I didn't believe such things happened at all. Not in *my* world.

And yet…two women were waiting for me at the station. I made a mental note to enjoy every second.

Carly greeted me on the platform, her yellow dress radiating sex. Our kiss was natural and expected and everything was just where we'd left it. It made me smile. I put my arm around her waist, and as we walked, she smiled and said, "Come on, Liz's waiting in the car!"

Oh yes. The second woman! A shiver of excitement ran through me. Somehow I wasn't nervous at all. How could I be anything but thrilled to be alive today?

I wondered if Liz would be nervous, and Carly confirmed as much.

After all, apart from anything else, she was married. I hadn't given that a lot of thought, actually. I was most certainly *not* someone to steal or use wives.

But this seemed entirely different. From what Carly had said, Liz and her husband had been to certain gatherings where he had allowed her to be penetrated by other men. And apart from that, she had been a serial cheat for some time, so any moral damage had been done already. I didn't see that taking the high ground was going to hurt anyone but me, in the circumstances. And this could be once-in-a-lifetime.

Still, she'd be nervous. So I surprised her when she pulled up to the pick-up zone. I opened the passenger door and, before I was even introduced to this completely unknown woman, I kissed her full on the lips. She laughed and smiled. And then said hello.

It was already turning into an unusual day.

We set off in the car, me and my two women. *Two* women! I was thoroughly hard, which wasn't about to change, and Carly knew it. She teased me, and Liz laughed some more, and I knew we were going to get along. There was no awkwardness happening in this vehicle.

Everyone agreed that sex on an empty stomach was not a good thing, so we took a detour to sate a different kind of hunger. Subway the establishment of choice. I pondered: something so mundane, *en route* to something so life-changing. Who else in the line for sandwiches was on their way to a threesome that morning? I loved that we had so saucy a secret, the three of us.

We giggled our merry way back to Carly's empty house. What a refreshing relief that they were as excited as I was. It helped that the two of them had played together before. They'd feed off each other's energy.

Carly had confided in me that she didn't really share the crush Liz had on her. But they were friends, and trusted each other, so Carly still enjoyed exploring her burgeoning lesbian side with Liz — priest's daughter and former Sunday School teacher — who was also experiencing a sudden burst of liberated behaviour in her late thirties.

We pulled up to the house and scuttled through the raindrops to the front door. Carly assured us the kids were all at school, but once again I locked the door behind us. Just to be safe.

Then, just as I'd done that, and Carly had put down her keys on the kitchen counter, a phone rang. It was Carly's cell. Her teenage son was calling from school. He wasn't feeling well, and wanted to come home on the bus. Now.

Please. God. No!

I held my breath, and I've never felt more selfish in my life. I exchanged a glance with Liz. She had that selfish look too.

Please don't take this away from me, kid.

Carly was taking a harsh line on the phone. She gathered it wasn't anything serious, and told him to see the nurse if it was. He protested a little.

"Look, you're not to come home," she said, frowning sternly at the phone. "Not on the bus. And I can't come and fetch you until school's out. Okay? It's gonna be fine, I promise."

She rang off, shaking her head. I stared at her, wide-eyed. Was he going to just come home anyway? Did he have a key?

"Yeah, he's got a key," she said, sounding more confident than I thought she should. "Come on, let's have a bath! I've got champagne guys..."

I shrugged, checked the front door once again, and followed her and Liz in the direction of what sounded like the *perfect* way to kick off a naughty morning on a rainy day. The spa bath was the en-suite to her seven-year-old daughter's room. Carly crossly tossed her child's strewn clothing out of the way as we passed through. *This is one naughty mummy...I like it...*

We closed the door and Carly began to fiddle with the taps, suggesting Liz and I undress each other. I liked how Carly was taking charge here. For the first time, I turned my attention to Liz, kissing the waiting, willing blonde woman before I did anything else.

How fantastic it was to know that this woman wanted to do things with me, long before I even arrived! What a moment to cherish! It was a different feeling to trying your luck and not knowing if the girl was going to slap you or not. I liked it. I could live with it being like this always.

Liz possessed a kissable mouth, gorgeous green eyes and soft, pleasant features. Sure, she was undeniably on the hefty side, but we were going to have fun today. I didn't care one bit.

I heard her suck in the air as I unbuttoned her blouse, unhooked her bra and sank my mouth onto her perky nipples. I liked them. They had a meaty texture and they were clearly excited. Invigoratingly suckable, with the odd little chew thrown in.

Her breasts were soft and warm and wonderful. The perfect handful. I barely noticed that the bath taps were now in full flow, and Carly had squeezed up behind me and begun unbuttoning my jeans.

This is it!! I wanted to keep this moment forever. I had the attentions of two women, and I was certain nothing could ever make me feel more beautiful. I'd put the moment in a museum if I could.

It wasn't going exactly as I had always dreamed, because that involved me watching them play together before they touched me. But hey, maybe this was better. It was most certainly *good*. Brain-explodingly good.

I felt Carly tug down my jeans, underwear and all, and Liz took the cue to sink to her knees. *Liz sucks cock very well.* The words had rung in my ears all week. Oh, and did she ever!

There it was again, that enthusiasm and pleasure and love for giving head. Except Carly was wrong: Liz wasn't *giving* anything. Just like with Carly, I could sense that she was *taking* something. This wasn't duty, this was her own wicked thrill, having her mouth filled with my erection.

And just like with Carly, Liz became a whole lot sexier at that moment. Knowing how much she wanted it made me feel guiltless about staying there all day. Meanwhile, I could feel Carly's hands and mouth roaming around my waist and my thighs. Had I ever been harder? With two women on their knees for me, that'd have to be a no.

Our little warm-up was over as quickly as it had begun, as Carly ordered us into the steaming bath. I noticed that she'd prepared three champagne glasses. There they were, lined up on the ledge. We shed what was left of our clothes, and I watched, enraptured, as the two naked girls climbed into the bubbles.

None of this seemed remotely possible. Was I really invited into a foamy bath with *two* cougars, lesbian lovers at that? One of whom I'd only met once, and the other only half an hour ago? With champagne? On a Wednesday morning?

Well, if it was a dream, I was going to enjoy it. A gigantic smile spread across my face. I love a bath with a girl. The cosier the better. *Two* girls? This might actually be better than the sex.

"Come on!" called Carly. "Stop dreaming…we need that cock in the water with us!"

"Yeah, get in here!" Liz giggled in agreement.

I shook my head, still in disbelief, but kept the smile. These wonderful, too-good-to-be-true women were giving me the happiest moment of my life. What an astounding thing the internet was! Only the World Wide Web, and its heaven-sent anonymity, could have united three kinky souls like ours with such ease.

They'd each nestled into one corner of the clover-shaped bath. I slowly lowered myself into mine. Our upper bodies may have had breathing space, but under the water it was a free-for-all of slippery legs. Is there anything better than skin contact tangled up in the embrace of warm water?

Carly handed us each a champagne glass, and we raised them as one. Glints in all six of our eyes. Their four nipples peeped above the surface as they held their drinks aloft, then disappeared from view as we all took a sip and sank back in blissful bubbles. I spread my legs, deliberately, so that each of my girls had a piece of me draped over them.

And because it's damn sexy spreading your legs. It invites so much. It proffers all of you.

Before long, a foot was softly nuzzling me there, sending my arousal into orbit. I wasn't sure whose it was — since each of them gave me a naughty look when I caught their eye — and I liked that. It heightened the *incredible* sensation of having two girls wanting to pleasure me. I lay back deeper and ran each of my wet feet over their respective nipples.

The bath was a nice idea, but all three of us were getting way too frisky to last long in there. We needed the master bedroom. All of it.

～

Carly lay spread-eagled and naked on her vast bed, and Liz was flicking her tongue over our gracious hostess's charged and deserving clitoris. Lesbian sex. *Right before my eyes.* The real deal. Porn could only hint at it.

No adult film could ever capture the energy these two were injecting into the room. Actresses could make all the right sounds, but I'd take the tiniest whimper of pleasure from Liz or Carly any day. With them, I knew the passion was real. Being there to share it, to feel it? Aah, this was privilege.

Before me was heaven, and I was more than happy to enjoy them enjoying each other for a while. No rush. But Carly would not let me spectate. The needy leader of our gang of three wasn't satisfied with just one playmate. Not when she could have two.

"Come on, bring that cock to my mouth, you!" she gasped in her don't-argue tone. "I want the best of both worlds!"

Oh, God, what sexy words. I forgot all about my plans to watch. Such enthusiasm, such craving, deserved everything I could possibly give her. *She was hugely turned on by the prospect of having me in her mouth.* I'd not known that feeling for three years! In fact, she'd already told me she'd been known to come from giving head alone. Truly a goddess!

I made sure to position myself so that I could see Liz's head working between her fuckbuddy's legs. And I got a little harder each time she flicked her gleaming, pure-filth eyes up to meet my gaze. Soon I couldn't get any harder if I tried. I was at full stretch. Life couldn't possibly get any sexier than this.

Except it did. At our next repositioning, I finally engaged both women at once. I knelt above Carly, who was back in her favourite position and still working my record-breaking erection with her wet, fun-loving mouth.

And Liz knelt too, pressed up against me, so that I might fondle her tits and kiss her. Which I did with pleasure that approached — then reached — the orgasmic. At just the right moment, I withdrew from Carly's mouth and dumped her favourite treatment on her.

She laughed and squealed and complained about her stinging eyes, wriggling herself upright, ready to dash for the running water across the hallway. But just as she swung her quivering legs over the edge of the bed, the fruit of her lust shot out of her without warning.

A monumental squirt burst forth from her red hot pussy. It rocked her — rocked all of us — with shock and surprise. Before any of us could take in what was happening, her stream of joy hit the carpet with splashes loud enough to rival the raindrops banging on the roof. Oh, we were brewing up a storm to be proud of in here!

Even Carly was taken aback for a moment, slamming a hand in front of her mouth. "Guys, I've never done that before!" she spluttered. "I don't know where it came from!" She shook her head in sheepish disbelief. "*Fuck!* You guys are doing something special to me here!"

Liz and I both grinned proudly at her as she ran off to clean up my cum from her face, and hers from her pussy and legs. I began to lap at Liz while the thoroughly sodden Carly was out of the room, wanting so much for our hostess to help me when she got back. Major fantasy: working a girl's pussy in tandem with another woman.

And we did it, too, pushing our heads into the tight space like greedy farm pigs gobbling at a trough. I loved the shared passion and the shared goal. I loved the way our tongues interlaced as we both probed that engorged clit and those slick lips, pleasuring each other while pleasuring her. I loved that I could learn the ropes from a woman at close quarters.

I loved that we were doing something we both loved and shared in common. It's why bisexual women are such a thing for me: if we both like girls then that's one more thing we both like. Shared passions are good.

Carly's attention span is not long, though, and after a couple of minutes she told me to spin round. So I twisted into a 69 as instructed, but instead of Liz attacking me with her mouth again, Carly guided my hind quarters into the air. She proceeded to slap liberal quantities of baby oil onto my back-with-a-vengeance erection, rubbing it everywhere between my legs with an abandon to die for.

I almost lost focus at this beautiful distraction, but eventually I brought Liz to climax. I felt a gentle tremor pass through her body as she came. She'd had the odd bout of guilty nerves today, and decided she'd rather not do the intercourse thing, so I was glad we'd got her to relax this much. *We.* A woman and I! That *we* would never stop being sexy. Not when the job was this much fun.

I knew I'd be needing to penetrate the incorrigibly horny Carly pretty soon. I excused myself for a moment to wash that wonderful oil off, only because I knew it wouldn't get on well with a condom. I splashed down quickly in the shower, eager not to miss a thing.

A beautiful scene greeted me when I returned to the bedroom. They lay on their sides, legs intertwined, embracing, and locked in a passionate kiss. Ah...women kissing. Total sucker for it! The eyes-closed intimacy of it is as hot as any lesbian sex act on the list. I stopped breathing, like I'd just seen a snow leopard and didn't want to scare it off.

But they heard me, gave each other a wicked grin, and beckoned me to lie down in the middle of the bed. What did these two vixens have in mind now?

Quickly they ran round to the foot of the bed, then crawled back up the sheets, advancing in the direction of my loins. There was fire in their eyes of my two crouching snow leopards: what was happening now?

Shit! The one thing I'd forgotten to ask for!

A double blow-job.

I will never find words for this feeling. Such an outlandish fantasy that even I had barely ever thought about it. But these truly amazing women had thought about it all by themselves — good girls!— and at that moment I would have turned down the world for them.

It was so delectable, so indulgent, I had to fight not to feel guilty. I lay there with no role to play other than to watch as two adventurous, liberated, free-thinking females pleasured my shaft with their tongues and lips. Here, there and everywhere they went, but never forgetting to keep eye contact. I was the undisputed king of the world, and I didn't know what I'd done to deserve it.

This is as good as life gets. Enjoy it, man, enjoy it!

But so removed was this from anything I knew, I was barely programmed to know how to enjoy this. I was torn between losing myself in it, abandoning myself to it, and trying to record every second in my memory. How did one even process pleasure so deep?

I should have asked for a countdown, so I could savour the last seconds before they stopped. But I only had that idea later.

At the time, it was Carly who pulled away first. Of course it was. She wanted fucking now. And I was certainly primed. A fucking is what she deserved, and a fucking is what she got. I took her from behind this time, while she bent over Liz and kissed her like crazy.

Both of us sprinted to another furious orgasm, and quickly we were a heap of hot, panting bodies. It was going to be at least fifteen minutes before I could go again with these two affectionate jackrabbits.

Then someone saw the time. *Three hours* had passed since we walked in the door! Kids! School! Appointments! *Fuck, fuck, fuck!*

I wanted to sleep all afternoon with them. And every night, forever. But real life had poked its nose in once again.

Not before my dream had come true, though. A broad-daylight dream whose delights went a thousand times beyond every depravity and pleasure my brain had ever concocted.

And a dream in which I learned that it was attitude and spirit, not looks, that made a woman a sex goddess. I lesson I would never forget.

HOT WET TOUCHES PART II

Jake froze on the spot. His lips fell open, suddenly dry. A sharp intake of breath. No exhale. Someone had just hit the pause button on his life. Everything went into suspended silence — but for the torrential swish of shocked adrenaline that was rushing through his system.

Only one person could do *that* to him. But surely he had to be mistaken? No way. No way in hell! And yet...yes!...it was *her*!

He kept on staring, like a saint transfixed by some divine apparition. She was gazing out of the café window. Hadn't noticed him yet. The nose stud settled his last, lingering doubts. It was *definitely* her. In a city this big, it was barely believable. Maybe he shouldn't allow himself to believe it.

But there she was! Mistaken identity just wasn't possible. Not when it came to *her*. Not for Jake. He had ogled this impossibly beautiful woman mercilessly that day. Feasted his eyes on her until they burned. Her image was stamped onto his brain with a sizzling brand. He was certain of that, because it hadn't left his head for four months.

Since their moment in the sauna, hardly a waking hour had gone by without the mystery stranger swimming, naked and shimmering, into his thoughts. He wasn't used to anyone having a hold on him like that.

He'd tried everything to shake her ghost. Back in his real world, in Canada, the good-looking Jake could pick up girls almost at will. He'd slept with several since Christmas. And they had done nothing for him. He'd felt like he was going through the motions. He'd wake up the morning after with no thoughts at all about his latest conquest. They were always drifting to *her*.

Guilty, stolen memories. But oh so vivid. Even after all this time. He'd check to see if his most recent one-night stand was awake, then figure out how to get her out of his bed so he could get back to daydreaming about that darn German. The whole thing had been driving him crazy.

He'd been back to Frankfurt twice on business in that time, but those trips had been flat-out busy. Not that he wouldn't have made time to work his magic on her — if he could find her. But that was just the thing. He didn't know her name. He didn't have a photograph of her. He didn't even know if she lived here — maybe she'd been an out-of-town visitor that day too? He'd resigned himself to feeding off her memory forever.

It was all too hopeless. Jake wasn't used to feeling this powerless when it came to the opposite sex.

Maybe that's why she was so damn alluring. He could have her, he was sure. She *might* have a boyfriend, but he sure hadn't gotten that vibe when he watched her with her friends that day. She had that particular slant of self-consciousness single girls have, and he trusted his instincts on that. So if she had found someone, he had to be pretty fresh on the scene. Fresh enough that she would be easy to sway.

But he *couldn't* have her, because he'd never find her again.

So he'd buried himself in his work, even tried some meditation stuff to stop himself thinking about what he'd do with her if he could just...*find* her.

And now, it looked like she'd wandered across his path. Here she was. Staring dreamily out of the window, munching on a croissant, flakes of pastry sticking to her lips. Alone.

Was this really happening? Or was he still in bed, a victim of his subconscious once again?

"Bitte?"

The cashier's voice startled Jake back into the present. To wide-awake reality. To his morning of wall-to-wall meetings, the first of which was bearing down on him.

"Sorry," he smiled, gathering himself. He was sure the woman at the cash register could hear his heart thudding away. *"Entschuldigung,"* he corrected himself. German practice was coming along well, but sometimes he forgot.

"Kein Problem," said the cheery woman, chuckling openly as she took the five Euro note from him and handed him his coffee. She'd seen how her customer had suddenly fallen under the spell of that pretty young girl in the far corner window.

Had he really been that obvious?

Well, this was a shock to the system! One seriously early start. Claudia was well into the second week of her Easter vacation, back home from college and sleeping once again in the room she'd occupied as a child. And she'd clearly gotten rather too accustomed to her holiday lie-in.

Today, though, she had an interview. It was for a summer internship. She wasn't feeling all that motivated right now, truth be told. She wasn't even sure business management was the field of study for her. She felt kind of stupid in this knee-length skirt and white blouse. It was all far too grown-up and serious. Especially at this hour of the morning.

The coffee was helping her perk up though. And eating a little something had been a good idea. A few bites into the gooey, crumbling chocolate croissant, it occurred to her that bringing a toothbrush might have been advisable too. She sighed at her own incompetence. She wasn't cut out for real life, she was quite sure of that. None of these working people, scurrying up the Kaiserstraße from the station, looked like they were having much fun. But they did look like they knew what they were doing.

That was pretty much it as far as Claudia's thoughts went that chilly Wednesday morning. She was still only semi-awake, not up for much more than resting on her elbows as she stood at the window bar, sipping her Americano. At least she'd left herself plenty of time. Thanks mainly to her mom's annoyingly reliable wake-up service. That woman wasn't familiar with snooze buttons at all.

She was so lost in thought that she didn't even hear the footsteps behind her. Nor did she even sense somebody standing close. It was, after all, a busy time of day at this popular on-the-run breakfast spot. And Claudia wasn't terribly switched-on at the best of times. She only woke up when a slip of paper, slid across the countertop by a hand, came into her peripheral vision. She looked up in surprise.

The stranger who'd slipped her the note turned out to be a tall, handsome-looking man. Very attractively built, actually. He was smiling a coy smile that made her pulse quicken. He was smartly groomed and expensively attired. She was too taken aback to say a word, but the man put a finger to his lips anyway, urging her silence. Claudia found herself transfixed to his brown, soulful eyes. Sucked in further by his dazzling scent, she obeyed his signal for quiet without a thought.

The stranger didn't take his eyes off her for a single second. Or…did she *know* him? Not well, obviously, but…? Then he pressed the little scrap of paper right into her hand. Lightly brushed her fingers as he retreated. She felt an inexplicable ripple of excitement at the touch.

And then he was gone. Claudia was alone with her breakfast once more — just like she'd been half a minute earlier. Did that encounter really happen? Was she dreaming? It was less than an hour, after all, since she'd been fast asleep in bed. She and this fine-looking visitor had locked eyes for what, ten seconds?

It definitely wasn't someone she recognised. Not consciously anyway. And yet…there was something about the way he approached her. Something different from the average guy just trying his luck. Some kind of certainty. The kind that goes with familiarity.

She gathered her wits just in time to turn around and see the guy push the door open and walk into the street. He didn't pass in front of her window but went off in the other direction — towards the biggest, tallest office towers in the city. She could only see the back of his bobbing head as it disappeared into the throng of pedestrians.

Only then did she turn her attention to the little square of paper nestling in her hand. It was crisp and thick, more like card. Bright white, no ruled lines. Tangible. Physical. *Real.*

She held her breath as she unfolded it and read the words. English words, written in blue ballpoint.

'Remember December? Same sauna. 7.45pm. Tomorrow evening.'

Claudia's hands began to shake. And it sure wasn't interview nerves.

Jake's heart pounded as he pushed his way through the crowd on Kaiserstraße. He was a naturally fast walker, and he found himself moving quicker than ever now. Some part of him wanted to turn back and undo what he'd just done. But no way was he going to let that part win.

The move he'd pulled back in the café was audacious even by his standards. He didn't like to think about it too much, but couldn't help himself. There were so many reasons not to do it. It was stalkerish. Maybe cheesy. Clichéd, even. Or was it? Maybe it was brilliant and original. The stuff of movie scripts. All he knew for sure was he would have died if he'd walked out of there without doing something. It might have been his only chance — ever.

His mouth curled in a self-congratulatory smile. Yeah, the way he did it might be open to criticism. But it took balls, and he was happy that his were still in fine form. There would have been *no way* he could look himself in the mirror if he'd let that sweet, gorgeous stroke of fortune go.

His options had been limited, after all. Writing and delivering that note had taken a minute he actually didn't have right then. He couldn't risk getting into a conversation when he was running as late as he was, so Jake was pretty pleased to have come up with some kind of plan on the fly.

The only mistake he'd made, now that he thought about it, was that he hadn't put his phone number down. He gave himself a little shrug as he pushed past a couple of worse-for-wear backpackers still busy with last night's partying. Maybe it was better that way. It meant she couldn't say no.

If she already had something arranged for the evening in question, there was time enough to change it. That's why he'd written 'tomorrow' instead of 'tonight'. Plus, it would give her a night to lie in bed thinking ahead to the next evening — whatever that might hold. He hadn't really had time to think as far as what he was going to do when the moment came. But he too had a night to dream up a scene.

She'd be there, though. He was pretty sure of that. The whole thing was just too romantic. A girl would need a heart of iron to decline an invite like that, no matter how many reservations she brought with her.

Yeah, she'd be there.

Claudia fluffed her interview completely. That otherworldly breakfast encounter had thrown her mind into disarray. A fog of thoughts and memories whirled through it. Mostly memories. *Him!* Back like a ghost from her past! Did she 'remember December'? Christ above, how could she ever forget it?

She didn't actually let any of those wicked, salacious memories cross her mind during the grilling itself, but her profound unsettlement still got the better of her. She fell over her words, spoke too fast, didn't listen to questions properly. She was a shy, nervous girl at heart, and seeing what felt like ghost a few minutes before her arrival was not something she handled well.

She was supposed to care deeply about the disappointment of seeing that tell-tale, polite, pursed-lips smile and hearing a curt, crisp 'thank you, we'll be in touch' before showing herself out of the interview office. She knew her chances weren't great, and that she was supposed to be miserable about it.

Instead, all she could do on the train ride home was read *that* note. Over and over and over. If it wasn't right there, in her hand, she'd be quite sure she'd fabricated the whole thing in her head. Even now, she was wondering. Maybe it was someone else who'd seen them misbehaving in the sauna? A practical joker? After all, she'd assumed the guy didn't even live around here. He sure wasn't local, or he'd have spoken German to her when he'd told her to leave the sauna. And she wouldn't be looking down at a note in English right now.

Her brow furrowed. Things added up rather too well for practical joker theories to work. Occam's razor: the simplest explanation was probably the correct one. Or something like that. And although this chance encounter — or *had* it been chance? — was unlikely, it was still more likely than anything else.

She squirmed in her seat and tried not to think about his fingers inside of her, that freezing day just before Christmas. She began to feel extremely uncomfortable, and just a touch damp. At least the train was nearly empty, heading away from the city centre as it was.

It would be so much easier to process this if she'd seen him properly the first time around. It had been so dark in that hot-house. She really hadn't been able to see him. All she had in her mind was a silhouette. But undeniably, that silhouette had been built much like the athletic man who'd approached her at the café this morning. She'd pondered whether her wandering mind had embellished the silhouette in the months since that afternoon, but his appearance today suggested not.

Now she knew just what this guy looked like: handsome, tall and manly. She didn't know his name. She didn't have his number. All she had was a time and a place. A place they both knew *very* intimately. Butterflies stirred deep inside her, flying figure-of-eight aerobatics in her stomach.

She pulled out her phone. What did her diary have in store for tomorrow? She noticed her hands were still shaking as she tried to unlock her keypad. Oh yes, lunch with the girls. But in the evening…nothing.

Claudia swallowed hard and folded her phone away again. She'd have to think about this properly. What did he want from her? Could it be…the same again? But what *else* could it be? She closed her eyes and shook her head, still reeling from the morning's events.

Yes, she'd definitely have to think about this particular invitation. If and when she finally stopped quivering.

Jake was struggling, big time. Still almost 24 hours to go! He lay on his bed and tried to watch television, but he found himself constantly eyeing the digital clock beside it instead. 8pm — this time tomorrow! Waiting was torture.

This quiet night in thing really wasn't working out for him. It had been a *long* day — one that began with an emotional explosion — and he was feeling drained. But now, fed and watered, with nothing but his fantasies filling his head, he wondered if he should have taken his client for dinner after all. This was getting painful.

What had he had in mind when he wrote that note, anyway? His wicked subconscious left him in no doubt what it wanted. He couldn't shake his visions of finishing off what he'd started last year. He'd made her come, and though it had been delicious for him to pleasure her that way, his selflessness had left him with a terrific longing. Longing that was manifesting itself in a stew of devilish thoughts right now.

Distracted, he flicked off the television with the remote. He might just as well stare at the ceiling. This brooding wasn't like him at all. His *modus operandi* right now would normally be to head out to a bar, either with his local associates or alone. He didn't mind going solo — he'd usually get chatting to someone over a frothy mug of German brew. Often a girl or two. And then one thing would lead to another.

But Jake didn't feel like talking to any girls tonight. Or anyone, for that matter. All he wanted to think about, talk about, fantasise about, was seeing *her* again. Lightly touching her milky skin, moist with the lightest beads of sweat. And he couldn't exactly talk to anyone about that. Except himself. These thoughts were driving him crazy.

The more erotic imagery flashed through him, the more he felt like this was a bad idea. It was going to take some kind of monkishness not to succumb again. Which might be fine at her place or his — but now he'd gone and arranged a meeting at the scene of the crime! Another naked meeting, whether she liked it or not. Sauna rules were still sauna rules. Which also meant no sex acts. In theory.

This was going to be the weirdest date ever.

Claudia was thinking, hard. Luckily her mom had gone out, so she could sit in peace, trying to order her thoughts. She'd made herself another coffee, and was sitting in her favourite spot at the corner of the kitchen table. Her brow was still creased, but it only made her prettiness more endearing. Not that the naturally modest, self-deprecating student knew it.

The analytical, conservative German in her was trying to win over her romantic side. It shook its head angrily and told her that all of this was entirely *verboten*. She may have broken the rules last time and gotten away with it, but she wouldn't be so lucky if she dared it again. And besides, careful girls like her didn't volunteer themselves for this kind of thing. Last time was a chance occurrence, a slip-up in the face of passion. This would be premeditated. Which would be entirely different.

But the red-blooded woman in Claudia wanted to argue back. 'Things like this don't happen in real life!' it protested. 'This is like a movie plot, and you're the heroine for once! Who walks away from a script like this? You'd have to be made of stone.'

'Yes,' said the analytical auntie within her, 'But you *do* know the script is going to run out, don't you? You really think you'll get an empty sauna yet again? Try something again, and you'll be caught and thrown out! You'll be in the newspapers, you slut! And you don't even know this guy's name, or anything about him. Who else has he been with? *Slut!*'

'Ah yes,' retorted Claudia the blind, heated optimist, 'But could anything be more romantic? You know, going back to the same place, still as strangers! After all these months of replaying *that one time* in your mind. After all these months of hard studying and no men worthy of mention. And he's so...hot!

'So what!' argued cold-hearted Claudia. 'There are plenty of attractive men out there. You don't have to hand yourself over to them, naked and in a public place. No gentleman would ask that of you.'

'Oh yeah?' Romantic Claudia was putting the hearts and flowers to one side. And she was getting aggressive now. 'Well, *actually* it takes some kind of gentleman to finger-fuck a lady like that with no thought for his own pleasure. In fact, come to think of it, you owe him one!'

There was a pause as turned-on Claudia succumbed to a quick, dirty hallucination. She was back in that sauna, bent over with her forearms resting on the knee-high lower shelf. And she was letting him have his way with her from behind. Violently hard, with the urgency that comes with fear of discovery.

At this thought she closed her eyes, ran her hands through her hair and inhaled sharply. A tightening of tiny muscles between her legs.

Then boring Claudia switched off the cinema screen in her brain and put on a new film reel. One where somebody walks in, gasping *'Mein Gott!'* as she and the sexy stranger are caught *in flagrante delicto*. They look in shock, too stunned to say anything. But then it goes off-script. The guy keeps pumping her. It's too late anyway. What's done is done. Let them take her away in shame. She orgasms in a frenzy of screams.

Hot, wet Claudia felt a proud and strange excitement welling up deep in her belly. She never knew she had it in her. She knew she'd won this argument with herself. For now anyway.

Careful Claudia shrugged, walked away from the kitchen table and let herself out. She knew she was fighting a losing battle with her silly other half. Maybe she'd try again later.

Jake had a quieter schedule the next day. He'd not had much sleep, kept up as he was by endless fantasies and visions. He'd felt a cruel longing for much of the night, begging the hours to tick by and the next day to succumb to the sands of time.

As Thursday went on, though, he pulled himself together and felt a little more like his old self. He had just enough work to keep him busy, yet little enough to allow himself the occasional reverie. Just enough human interaction to keep him sane, but enough alone time to allow him to form a plan for the evening.

She would be punctual. She was German, and Germans are as reliably on-time as their trains and their trams. And she would definitely remember where to go. No way could anybody walk out of an experience like she'd had without every detail etched into their being.

He wanted to be there before her. He sensed she was shy and that he would be expected to take the lead. He was fine with that, but he would need to assess the lay of the land with a clear head. Which he most definitely hadn't had the last time he was in that roasting little cabin with her.

It may have been accidental, he thought to himself, but he had proposed a time that would be great for privacy. Most people would be having dinner in the restaurant, taking a break from the delights of the spa before a final sweat for the night. But even at that hour an empty sauna was by no means guaranteed.

If they did turn out to be alone, then Jake was going to have an extraordinarily hard time restraining himself. Of course, her being up for finishing what they had started was another thing he couldn't guarantee. Women were weird sometimes. She'd probably overthink everything, and come up with some reason why it was now a bad idea.

But again, if she turned up, then…after what happened last time…it would have to be a pretty good sign.

Still, the usual physical signals weren't going to be much use. Back home, if a girl walked naked into a room then…well, he would know what she wanted! But in an all-nude spa, she'd have to be naked regardless of what was going on in her mind. Even if she just came out of curiosity, hoping to find out his name.

Part of him hoped that's exactly how it would be. He wasn't in the usual run of things a guy for sex in public. The fear of getting caught did little for him. Yeah, the idea of a repeat of December's antics tickled him a bit, but in reality wouldn't it just be pushing the good luck too far? Even just using the sauna as a meeting point would still be a great storyline — perhaps one that involved dinner and then the privacy of his hotel room.

On the other hand, he'd always believed that he should take a chance when it was there. *Carpe diem.* Just like he had done in the café the morning before. If he hadn't seized *that* day, his evening would be looking a lot less intriguing.

If there were people inside the sauna at the time they were set to meet, then that would be that. He'd have to smile, take her outside, and they'd have to talk properly. Like civilised adults, not like rutting animals.

If the sauna was empty…well, who could say?

His head pounded at the prospect and he looked at his watch.

Quarter to five.

~

Well, *this* was ironic.

Lunch with Rosa and Corinne was another coincidence Claudia just couldn't have scripted. The same two school friends who'd joined her at the spa that electric day at Christmas time. The same two school friends who'd left her to her delicious fate when the heat in that sauna became too much.

Everything seemed meant to be. Somehow pre-ordained. Were the stars aligning this Easter?

Claudia had resolved to keep the whole thing to herself. Tonight's crazy *rendez-vous* would give her friends too much teasing ammunition. Plus, it was scarcely believable anyway.

A glass of wine, though, and more stories of Corinne's prowess with boys in the semester just finished, to which Claudia had nothing to contribute, changed her mind. That, and the embarrassing subject of her sauna sex coming up again.

It had been coming up ever since December, really. Every time she'd spoken to either of them. She couldn't blame them — it was outstanding ribbing material and they were good-natured about it. But part of her wished she hadn't spilled the beans after staggering out of that hot wooden room.

"What shall we do the rest of the week, ladies?" said Corinne. Then, with a wicked grin, she added: "Maybe Claudia would like to go back to the spa…?"

"Hah, she might find it a disappointment this time around," joked Rosa.

"Who knows, maybe her guy will be there again?"

Claudia started to go bright puce, and looked around the restaurant to see if anybody was listening. But the nearby tables had cleared out — this was nothing if not a lingering lunch, and it was nearly three o'clock.

"No, he's from somewhere else in the world, isn't he Claudia?" Rosa stuck out her bottom lip, aping a child's sad face. The gesture came across as more than a little mocking.

Claudia snapped suddenly. Partly irritation, partly the pleasure of telling them.

"Maybe…but you want to know something weird? I saw him in town yesterday!"

Now even Corinne was speechless. Claudia looked at her friends, and both were dumbstruck. They looked quite goofy, really. Why did something good happening to her always seem to shock them so?

Corinne spoke first: "You…wait, hang on, say that again?"

Rosa looked on, wide-eyed and fascinated.

Claudia felt the flush burning her temples. Was it hot in here? She took her hands off the table so she'd stop playing with them.

"I said I saw him yesterday morning. The guy from the sauna…here, look…"

She reached into her handbag and pulled out the note. She unfolded the paper — so laden with promise — and smoothed it out on the table so they could read. Her friends leaned in to examine it.

"Nooo way!" whispered Rosa, looking up at Claudia and staring at her.

Corinne just shook her head.

"Come on, girl…you never were any good at practical jokes. And April the first was last week!"

Rosa punched Corinne playfully: "Aw come on, you, how do you know she's kidding?"

"You're right," said Claudia with mock huffiness. "I'm not a joker, am I?"

She looked Corinne straight in the eye as she said this, and her face didn't crack.

"Jesus, she's serious!" Corinne went all slack-jawed again. "How in the world…?"

Claudia shook her head slowly and shrugged with her face.

"He saw me in a café when I grabbed a quick breakfast. I didn't recognise him because, you know…it was dark that time. But who else could write that note?"

The girls all paused for thought. Nobody could come up with an answer to her question.

"And he *is* pretty handsome," Claudia resumed with a note of satisfaction in her voice. "Very beautiful in fact."

More silence, as her friends digested this information. Claudia took the last swig of her wine and awaited a response.

"So, you *are* going…right?" asked Corinne, raising her eyebrows, an almost threatening note in her voice.

Claudia didn't have to say it. Her mouth twitched as she tried to suppress a smile.

Rosa gasped and Corinne clapped her hands like a thrilled child. Mocking time was over.

"This is SO exciting! What a story! I want to know what happens! Hey Rosa, do you feel like going to the spa tonight?"

"Don't you two dare even think about it!" Claudia growled. The very idea made her hair stand on end.

Her friends sighed, then smiled.

"Okay, okay, we'll stay home!" smirked Corinne. "But I want every detail in the morning. You'd better call me!"

"Yes, Mom," laughed Claudia, feeling a little more relaxed for having the whole thing off her chest. It wasn't the sort of thing she could tell her real mother, that was for sure. "I have to go and get ready now…"

"Well, it won't take long… you won't need to worry about what clothes to wear!" chirped Rosa with a chuckle. It was unusual for her to come up with a line like that. Normally Corinne would get there first.

Claudia didn't answer. She just went crimson once more.

Jake couldn't wait for his work day to end. He grabbed a quick hot dog in the station before boarding a train that would get him to the spa at least an hour ahead of his date with destiny. He didn't want to be hungry, after all. He might need energy.

His appearance was ruffled after a day on the go, but Jake had decided not to shave before making the short walk from his hotel to the station. Stubble suited him and his strong jawline. He didn't have to worry about his hair: the tousled, scruffy look always seemed to ignite women as much as careful grooming did. His calming brown eyes would come with him whether he liked it or not. And he wouldn't need to worry about clothing when he saw her.

How weird to show up for a meeting naked! Even if you called it a date. But he'd packed some top-quality cologne, hair wax and a decent change of clothing for afterwards. Just in case. That was pretty much every base covered.

Really, he only needed to clean himself up — and there'd be plenty of time at the spa for that. It would give him something to do besides eyeing girls. Although this time around, he might not be doing much of that. His mystery lady's presence in his mind was already doing things to the crotch of his pants. The last thing he'd need at the *Therme* would be other hot young things to run his eyes over. Not when he was this coiled.

He just wanted to see her now. That was the main thing. Sure, he'd had many a sordid thought about finishing what he begun all those months ago. But he also knew that the act itself could wait if it had to. He was absolutely *not* going to leave the spa without her name and contact details. That was priority number one.

Reflecting on that subject, the horrible notion began to dawn on him that she might have something really important in her diary this evening. Something she couldn't cancel. A graduation, or a wedding... or a three-month anniversary date with her boyfriend. He didn't like that last thought, nor the fact that she had no way of contacting him to reschedule.

He knew she'd want to come back. He just had a sense about that — he was pretty intuitive when it came to reading the opposite sex. It just worried him that maybe she *couldn't*. Oh, why hadn't he been smart enough to leave his number?

He shifted uncomfortably on his train seat. Roll on seven forty-five.

~

"Cuckoo, I'm home Claudia!"

Mom! Claudia sighed and rolled her eyes as she heard the front door close, a jangling of keys and that unmistakable clumsy bustling in the hallway. Another half an hour, and she could have left without being quizzed about where she was heading. Being back with her parents for the holidays had made one thing clear to her: living at home after graduation wasn't an option. She'd go crazy in three days. She'd gotten used to her independence now.

She wasn't going to say anything about going to the *Therme* alone. Her mother was a real fan of the place, and was usually there two or three times a month, absorbing all the good it did for her skin and sense of wellness. They'd soaked there together more than once: mom very definitely saw it as a social activity.

Claudia didn't want questions: she didn't think well on her feet and tended to get caught out when she made up fibs. Should have left earlier, she thought to herself. Should have just gone for a drive to kill the time. It wasn't as though she didn't have plenty to think about.

Now she was paying the price for pottering around in her room, thinking of everything and nothing. She'd just about managed to scratch together a kit bag, but it hadn't been easy. Sensible Claudia was back, making a final round of pleas, but couldn't get so much as a word out of naughty Claudia, preoccupied as she was with a warming feeling in her stomach and imagining herself peeling off her towel and pushing open that sauna door.

Damn, the kit bag! *That* was one thing she'd have done well to think more carefully about. Now a smothering inquisition from mom was going to be all but inevitable, and any lies would have to be more carefully considered. She castigated herself for not thinking to put it in her car a little earlier.

'Really, you're quite hopeless,' Claudia thought to herself. 'You'd be the worst spy ever!'

She was no closer to a plan of action when she heard her mom clumping up the stairs to find Claudia sitting on her bed, making a very poor job of looking occupied.

"You look bored, dear!" smiled her mother. "Are you feeling all right? Did you have a good lunch?"

She was a sweet lady, Claudia knew that. Just a little overbearing. Claudia was an only child, and it was hard not to feel claustrophobic. Especially after being away from home for so long now.

"Yes, it was very nice, thanks, Mom," she replied, trying not to sound breathless, nor give a hint of being in a hurry. Nor bored, either. Her mother and her questions might be unstoppable if she picked up on anything like that.

"I had an idea you might like," her mother went on. "Unless you're doing anything with your friends tonight?"

Panic rose inside Claudia. What to say? Her eye caught her wall clock: it was twenty past six. Not much more than an hour, and he'd be waiting for her. Unless her mother was going to ruin everything.

Her mom ploughed on before Claudia could answer.

"I thought maybe we could go to the *Therme*? Just you and me…it's been such a long time."

Claudia's heart started thudding at the very mention of the spa. Cold blood this time. The minute hairs on her delicate forearms stood on end. This couldn't be happening! Of all the days in the year! Inside her head, she screamed with frustration. Which didn't leave much room for thinking of a response to her interfering, infuriating mother.

"Claudia? So what do you think?"

Her daughter was befuddled. If she said she was busy with her friends, that might work, but she hated lying. And it would probably backfire somehow. If she said yes, her mother would probably hold her up, thinking there was no rush to get there. Respectable Claudia perked up at the thought that mom's presence might stop her doing something silly again. Oh, but wicked Claudia didn't want that! The muddle of thoughts snowballed inside her brain.

"Uhm…sure?"

She heard the words come out of her mouth. It was too late now. Wicked Claudia wanted to slap that pretty mouth, hard. What a stupid thing to say! Why didn't she just LIE? Had decent, truthful Claudia just gone and ruined everything?

Her mother clapped her hands, just as Corinne had done — for far less savoury reasons — earlier that afternoon.

"Okay, my treat! I'll drive us! Have you eaten? We can eat there, spoil ourselves a little!"

Claudia frowned and sighed as her mother walked away in the direction of her room. Then she had an uncharacteristically lucid thought. She sprang up from her bed and popped her head out of the doorway.

"Can we leave soon, mother? I'm really very hungry!"

Jake didn't feel his usual spa self this time around. Normally he'd be hyper-excited by his surroundings. The dozens of naked women, to be precise.

Tonight, even though it was busy in the co-ed changing room, he had bigger things on his mind. Or just one big thing, really. The stranger's amazing body. Those soft, feminine, creamy breasts and their roseate nipples, which he remembered like he'd seen them yesterday. He was rapidly losing his cool. But trying to think of something else was easier said than done.

Perhaps a cold shower would help.

He stripped off and stuffed his gear into his locker. Unusually, he'd hired himself a bathrobe and — even more unusually — he put it on right away. Normally he'd revel in the thrill of being naked as much as possible, and a drying towel was all he would take. In the ordinary course of events, he'd keep that thrill — and hence any danger of an embarrassing erection — under control.

He wasn't confident of that kind of control tonight.

He shook his head as he walked through to the shower area. It was weird to be back. It was about the fifth time he'd been here, but the first time since *that* time. Everything was familiar, yet so different. The customary sight of naked men and women, all shapes and sizes, greeted him as he entered the *textilfrei* area. Even after a few visits, that moment always struck him as incredibly foreign.

So far things looked normal. It was reasonably busy. He could hear showers running, see comings and goings from the indoor saunas. A handful of meditative people occupied the indoor bubble baths.

Any moment alone with her tonight would need a lot of luck, he thought to himself.

The cold shower did help a little. He found himself staring at the floor, rather than checking out any of his neighbours in the open-plan. It was decidedly odd behaviour for Jake. But his brain was fully occupied, oscillating between thoughts of his *rendez-vous* and trying *not* to think of his *rendez-vous*. He washed himself absent-mindedly up and down. He left his hair dry: you couldn't play around with hair wax in the wet area.

He took particular care washing his groin. He gently massaged the soap along his length with his hand, then lathered up his balls and ran a cleansing finger even lower. And suddenly he wasn't feeling so absent-minded any more. God, there was only one place for his manhood right now, he thought as he turned to the tiled wall to shield his growth.

For all he knew, *she* could be here early too. She might turn up in the shower next to him, though he suspected her shyness would make her hide rather than do that. Still, it was an exciting thought. One that he had to stamp on the head. He could not get himself any more aroused right here. But it was becoming a difficult struggle.

He looked at the nearest gigantic analogue clock mounted on the wall. There were always plenty of those around: Germans liked timing things to the minute. It read seven fifteen.

Much to her surprise, Claudia's spontaneous hurry-up tactic did the trick. Her mother managed to get herself ready by seven. The drive was probably 20 minutes, traffic permitting. Not much margin for error, she thought to herself as her mother clucked and cooed around the dogs one last time, oblivious to Claudia's tapping foot. But she wouldn't be disastrously late — yet.

And what was she going to be disastrously late for? Oh yes, the weirdest date ever. Walking into a sauna, naked, to meet a man who'd fingered her to the orgasm of her life last year. A man whose name she didn't even know. And a sauna that might be occupied by others. She shook her head to herself, wondered if she'd really be brave enough to push open that door. Claudia was beginning to have serious doubts on that.

But she was pretty sure she *did* want this encounter. Wherever it might lead. If only she could get her mother out of the house in time!

"Come on mom!" she said through clenched teeth, unable to hide her irritation. "I'm really hungry," she added with a tense little grimace.

"Okay, yes…what's the matter with you tonight? You really are very antsy!"

Maybe that's because I might be about to do something unspeakable that I can't talk to you about. And you've decided you're coming with me. God!

"I'm fine," Claudia answered with a weak smile. "But can we go please?"

After what seemed an eternity, they were on the road. Claudia's heart was beating so loudly she felt sure her mother would hear it over the Chopin studies that were the music of choice in this vehicle. The sound of gifted fingers crashing their way all up and down a piano keyboard wasn't exactly calming for her. But at least there weren't any soppy lyrics to freak her out. Maybe Chopin was for the best.

She could feel herself getting hotter, and began to fear that she'd break out in a sweat. Surreptitiously she inspected her reflection in the side mirror: her face looked dry on the surface. Had she packed any moisturiser?

It was dark now. Claudia eyed the clock readout every minute. Seven seventeen. Seven eighteen. Seven nineteen.

She had had visions of getting there nice and early, maybe just relaxing in a pool or jacuzzi, so she could mentally prepare herself. Why exactly wasn't that happening? Oh yes…no good reason. Just disorganised Claudia winning out.

And now she was going to rock up in a hurry and a flap. No doubt looking a mess, though she'd found some time to untangle her hair and brush her teeth before leaving.

Seven twenty. Seven twenty-one.

Only now did the awful thought hit her that, having bellyached about food before leaving, she would logically be expected to sit down and eat in the spa restaurant before running off to a sauna. Oh, and then it would be eight o'clock before their order even arrived!

This was getting more and more complicated. Claudia closed her eyes and quietly took a deep breath. If her mother only knew of the noise going on in her little girl's head right now!

Claudia seriously began to think about dropping the whole thing and standing him up. It wasn't just that she wasn't feeling courageous, but this thing with her mom being there…and having to make up tales…it was all making her head spin.

She decided to take it as it came. She had no better ideas, but naughty Claudia was still desperate to find a way to make this work. The consequences of worst-case scenario simply didn't bear thinking about. But part of naughty Claudia squirmed a little at what that might mean.

Jake passed a few minutes in one of the bubbling hot tubs, his eyes closed, trying his best to think of nothing. It was no good. He knew there was every chance she'd be here by now, that she might float angelically past at any moment. He didn't particularly like the idea of catching her eye. Even for a confident guy like him, that would be awkward.

And it might spoil the fantasies she's been having. Don't want that. Keep to the script.

He opened one eye and glanced at the clock again. Seven thirty. OK, time for action! Now he felt a good kind of nervous: the waiting was almost over. Something exciting was about to happen, and not knowing how it was going to unravel had him smiling. At last! He was ready — and maybe it was good that his mind had enough practical concerns to stop thinking how sweet it would feel to press up against her from behind and nibble at her neck…

First, he had to cool down. Though he wanted to be in the sauna first, he was wary of being overheated by the time she arrived. Hyper-thermia might have played its part in their previous encounter, but there was a limit to how long anyone could stand it in there. Especially if there was a chance of something more…physical. It was one thing to gently rub a girl's pussy and massage her G-spot. It was quite another to do what he kept thinking of doing to her.

Yes, it would be best to start out as cool as possible. He resolved to spend a few minutes chilling — literally — in the garden. It was still only April, and an evil breeze had been swirling around the city all day. Jake wasn't surprised to feel it hit him again as he went out of the garden door.

Though a few heads bobbed in the swimming pool, sheltered from the wind by the lightly heated water surface, the garden was otherwise quiet. To his left was the restaurant terrace, but it looked like most people had shunned it tonight for an indoor meal. Through the window he could see that the main restaurant was packed.

Good. Less people out here, then. But the sauna at the bottom of the garden could be packed too, for all he knew.

What would he do then?

Jake hadn't really come up with a Plan B. His lush fantasies had kept taking hold of his thoughts and running away with them before he could reason sensibly in any direction.

He shrugged to himself once more. He'd work something out. He always did. He was beginning to feel more and more in his element now. A controlling leader would be needed any moment. And that was where he always came into his own.

He was cooling down very nicely now, as he contemplated the outdoor hot tub from where he'd spotted that bewitching goddess for the very first time. A moment in his life he would never forget.

The outdoor clock read seven forty.

He opened up his robe, just to get a final blast of cold air into his body.

He consciously stopped himself from looking around. He didn't want to spot her just yet. It would spoil his own fantasy too. Better the romantic meeting, arranged by a note scribbled hastily in a rush-hour café.

Silently he patted himself on the back for doing that.

It's time, he thought to himself.

Slowly, calm on the outside, Jake followed the garden path towards that sauna. He reached the bottom of the steps, took a deep breath and opened the outer door.

He looked around the little antechamber where people left their flip-flops and robes before going into the sauna itself. His eye was on the lookout for the usual signs of occupation.

First, though, he noticed a little sign propped up on the window sill. It sported one simple German word: Aufguss. He'd seen signs like it before — he knew that at certain scheduled times this one would be hung on the sauna door to warn people that one of those curious towel-flapping heat sessions was on the go. That they shouldn't interrupt.

Then Jake looked down at the floor. Two pairs of flip-flops. Carefully placed in orderly fashion, beneath two white bathrobes hanging from the wooden pegs.

His heart sank at the evidence. It could mean only one teeth-clenchingly frustrating thing. There were people inside.

She was beside herself now. Ten minutes till her date with *him*; with the impossible. And she couldn't breathe a word about it. Inside, she was jumping up and down, edgy and snappy and excited and wanting to run away all at once. But on the outside the only hunger she could show was that for her dinner. But not *too* much. That could backfire.

The double act was already making her head hurt. Even as the butterflies zipped around in her belly. Claudia tried desperately to formulate some kind of plan as she and her mother entered the wet area in their bathrobes. Her mom had chattered away incessantly as they'd undressed in the locker room, and Claudia had found it impossible to zone her out. She simply couldn't think with all that noise going on.

'No wonder you're quiet,' she thought to herself as she surveyed the inside part of the spa from the corner of her eye. 'Your mother is so damn talkative. The next generation always rebels.' She flushed at the thought of another rebellion. But that of being a polar-opposite quiet daughter might look pretty good compared to the one she had in mind.

The clock on the wall read 7.38. Claudia's pulse took off like wildfire. She needed to take charge, and take charge now. How long would he wait if she didn't show on time? He'd just think she wasn't coming! The dull thud of her quickening pulse beat in her head too, like the soundtrack to some suspense thriller.

"To the restaurant then, my girl!" her mother sang. Really, that shrill voice was *not* what Claudia needed right now. "I promised to feed you up! I bet they starve you at university, don't they? Let's put that right. Come…this way!"

Claudia's resolve vaporised. It always did. How had she gotten herself into this awful situation? Silently she kicked herself as she blindly followed her mother through the spa, past the bathers in various states of undress, and into the dining area. Here, as was customary, everyone wore their robes to eat.

Her mother led her to what looked like the only remaining vacant table. Claudia picked up a menu, gazing at it through glazed eyes but seeing nothing. But she could feel it shaking in her hand. Her other hand went to her mouth, and her teeth began to chew on a nail. She hadn't done that since she was a child.

There could only be about four minutes to go.

"This salmon pasta looks good, you know. I think we had it before, didn't we? It was nice and creamy, if I remember."

Creamy. God, did her mother *have* to talk this way?

Something told Claudia it was time to go for broke. The timid Claudia she knew so well would probably have capitulated right about now. She'd just let events run away with her and give up, all passive and helpless.

But she had played so many scenes in her head now. Melded them with her montage of smouldering memories from that day. None of which seemed real any more. Another reason to go back to that sauna. Just to see if she'd gone crazy. That, and…what could happen. If she could only get there…then passive and helpless Claudia would do just fine.

"I think I need to go to the bathroom," she croaked, avoiding her mom's concerned eyes as she banished timid Claudia for this one crucial moment.

She needed more time! That little excuse wouldn't buy her enough minutes!

"And…I quite like the idea of a quick steam before eating," she added hastily as the skin around her throat tightened its grip. "I just feel a bit… sticky, you know?"

Some choice of words. Probably not far off the mark. She'd have smiled if she wasn't so tense.

And she prayed her mother wouldn't make it difficult now. She literally clasped her hands together under the table, pleading with any god that might listen.

Her mother looked a little surprised.

"I thought you were hungry, girl!" she replied.

"I am, but it will take a while for our order to come. And it's nice to eat clean. If you don't mind keeping the table for us while I go?"

Claudia summoned up her best pout. It felt watery and unconvincing, but her kind-hearted mother returned it and cocked her head.

"Of course dear, if that's what you want to do! It's my treat, after all. Let's just order before you go."

Suddenly it dawned on Claudia that she wasn't hungry. The whole impending-starvation ruse was ridiculous considering the substantial, late lunch she'd had with her friends. And the backflips her stomach was doing. She gave thanks that her mom was too busy chatting to have worked that out.

She pretended to deliberate over her meal choice. Claudia was a dreadful actress. But if she could only hide her excitement for a few more moments…if only her thrilled nerves didn't jump out of her skin at the realisation that she'd talked her way into a little time alone.

Thank God her mother seemed oblivious, deliberating over the menu again. It took several more minutes before Claudia could get away. But, after mumbling something about chicken salad to the waiter and flashing her mother another fake smile, get away she did.

Jake wasn't the sort of guy to wear a watch. Timepieces were just decoration as far as he was concerned. Another thing to get in his way all day. He had a strong natural sense of time anyway. And he knew it must be five minutes past their appointment now.

Where *was* she?

He eyed the middle-aged couple on the opposite side of the sauna with distaste. They were both laid out on their backs, eyes closed and dead to the world. He screwed up his face at them, and stuck out his tongue like a jealous, scowling schoolboy. He wanted them gone so bad. He wished he could tell them just how important their departure was right now.

They'd probably been coming here for years, he thought to himself. They were all about the stillness, the soothing calm, the health benefits. The *Wellness*, as the Germans liked to call it. Without a doubt, these two would be stern enforcers of *Ordnung* in a place like this. Order. Rules. The way things had to be. These were not people who could even conceive of doing what he'd done in here.

He'd been sitting in almost exactly this place. Middle shelf, to the left as you walked in the door. She'd been *there*. Oh *God*! The memory came rushing before his eyes, and he could see her beneath him, all glorious perfection, stretched out, impossibly beautiful, from the tiny ends of her molten-gold hairs to the tips of her toes. Those *breasts*. Those *sweet* nipples, all subtle and pink and just so damn *pretty*!

Jake was starting to harden as her soft, creamy image invaded the empty bench beneath him, refusing to go away. Oh boy. And he hadn't even started to think about the things he'd done to her. That deep-seated memory of her lying there — just lying there — was too much already. He leaned forward, shrouding his erection in the shadow beneath his clasped arms. Thank God the light was so dim in here.

The nondescript chestnut-haired woman opposite him cleared her throat and shifted slightly, but showed no signs of rousing herself. Jake rolled his eyes. Did she *know* how much she was getting in the way right now? Did her moustached husband have the foggiest clue? Of course not. To Jake the two of them looked so nondescript; so saggy and shabby. Neither attractive nor unattractive. Just people. But *he* had a heavenly creature waiting in the wings! An angel!

Or did he? In his reverie he'd forgotten that she was by now decidedly late. What was it about this place that made him lose his reason? He guessed it must be eight minutes past seven forty-five. So much for German punctuality.

As if to spite the rising heat and gentle perspiration, Jake felt a cold sweat at the thought that she wasn't going to arrive.

Claudia scurried to the toilet, a tingle radiating from the knots deep inside her. Time was precious now...why was she wasting it in here? She didn't even need the bathroom at all! Was she going to back out now? Naughty Claudia was tapping her foot impatiently, keeping time with her thumping heart beat.

Some feminine instinct made her examine her face in the mirror. As usual, she didn't think much of what she saw. Why was she so pointy? Her features were too sharp! And whose idea had that nose stud been? It really wasn't her style. Silly thing. Oh well, too late now.

Her hair was bunned up tight, as it always was when she came here. Not the greatest look, but neat at least. There wasn't a loose strand in sight — not since she'd pulled that hair firmly back across her scalp. But it made her forehead look big, didn't it? She was getting moody at her unsatisfactory appearance. Wicked Claudia shoved her out of the door before her thoughts got any darker.

She sighed as she padded carefully across the wet, slippery floor of the indoor bathing area. Though there was evidence of plenty of recent drips and splashes from the saturated patrons, it seemed like most people had retired to the restaurant now. God, did that mean the sauna would be empty?

Respectable, nervous Claudia desperately didn't want it to be empty. She was worried she might get overcome again. And that this time she'd get caught. His gorgeous face, which she'd only glimpsed so briefly yesterday morning, swam into her vision again. Damn, that didn't help at all.

She tried to look casual as she pushed the door into the garden area, relieved that her mother's seat was facing away from the window. She felt a surge of adrenaline as the cold air — and the unavoidable closeness of her destination — hit her face-on.

She was glad of her flip-flops and robe as she made her way down the garden path. Only now did it strike her that she would be naked in a matter of moments. It always took her a few moments to get used to that, but tonight she wasn't going to have that luxury before seeing him.

If he was even still there, that was. How late was she? Surely not more than ten minutes. He'd be getting hot by now. She'd ruined it! Whatever 'it' was…she was sure she'd spoiled everything.

Her legs turned to jelly as she stood at the top of the steps leading down to that sauna. She began to tremble, but forced herself to keep her feet moving. Each step she took was slow and deliberate, like those of a grandmother fearful of falling. Her teeth chattered and her temples throbbed. Every footfall felt like a victory on her wobbly ankles.

She couldn't turn back now. And she thought of the time. Whatever *he* had in mind, she knew she couldn't stay long. That thought helped her summon the strength to open the outer door…after all, what could go wrong in such a short space of time? Her head felt foggy as she entered the antechamber and saw the familiar, warm glow of the sauna room through the little window in the inner door.

Would he even be there? Maybe it really had been a nasty joke. Maybe she wasn't meant to take that note seriously at all.

Claudia's inner devil gave her a shove towards the final door and its smouldering secrets. Feeling faint, yet so alive, she slipped off her robe and hung it. Then she kicked off her flip-flops. She was completely naked now. Just like last time.

Thump. Thump. Thump. Her heart.

Cautious Claudia pushed the door open, as quietly as she could for fear of disturbing anyone inside.

Oh God. *There he was.* The first thing she saw as the door opened. She knew his shape in an instant. She felt everything inside her jump and churn as he looked up in her direction.

And wicked Claudia leapt for joy as he beckoned to her. Urgently.

Holy fucking shit — she made it! Jake had begun to prepare himself for disappointment. For the let-down of his life. But here she was! And she was just glorious. Absolutely drop dead glorious.

He'd often wondered if he'd been wearing rose-tinted spectacles on all the hundreds of occasions he'd drifted back to that December day. And yesterday's café encounter had been too much of a shock, too hurried, for him to decide either way. But now, ready and salivating for her appearance on the scene, he knew his memory had been true to him. It was still perfection that was peeping around this door. Perfection that revealed its naked flesh as she slid, shy and cautious, into the sauna.

Jake was only dumbstruck for a moment. He was usually good at thinking on his feet and — a little more prepared than last time — he found himself taking charge naturally enough. She looked nervous. Surprise, surprise! But she'd come to meet him, that was all that mattered. He would look after her now.

Instinct told him that the girl would be coy, riddled with doubts. So he signalled his recognition with a beckon as soon as she looked his way. It would reassure her and stop her worrying that she might have to decide what to do. He smiled too, but she might not be able to see that in this gloaming.

And he kept on beckoning, fearful she might lose her nerve. He summoned her and summoned her until she could no longer feel awkward. He gestured her to sit next to him, on his right hand side. She followed his directions without question, but cautiously. She took her place, but didn't sit too close. Certainly not touching.

He wasn't sure she'd noticed they had company. So for the second time in as many days, he put a conspiratorial finger to his lips, jerking his head to the comatose couple across the floor. She started as she followed his glance, then looked back at him. She was close enough now that he could see worry in her eyes. Then she looked away. Probably to hide her disappointment, he reckoned.

Jake found himself moving his finger from his own lips to hers, gently turning her chin with his other hand, so that she faced him again.

He stayed like that a while, enraptured by the simple intimacy of this gentle touch. She held her body absolutely still. He could feel her melting, and not just from the heat. Her lips quivered a little against his meaty index finger, and ever so slightly they opened.

Claudia whimpered a little as he withdrew his hushing finger. Then her heart sang as he moved in closer, whispered in her ear. No, it wasn't a whisper…what was softer than a whisper? It was a spoken breath, nothing more. Breath that was warm, moist and purposeful. Loaded with promise.

"Do you speak much English?"

He whispered the question.

She'd been trying to think in English ever since yesterday morning, to refresh her rusty high-school brain. She'd had little success. But she would get by. She absolutely would.

"Enough," she replied, nervous, leaning into his right ear. She wasn't keen to use a lot of words. She'd probably get them wrong, and anyway, they'd get ratted out by that couple if they made any noise.

They had moved closer to each other now. How else could they whisper that softly? His side touched hers as he leaned in again. *Ah!* The contact felt like hot sparks.

"You are so beautiful," he breathed once again.

Claudia reeled. The touch. The breath. Those words.

She smiled back at him, showing how much it meant. She wanted to say it back, and more, but she didn't trust herself to be quiet enough. Or to control herself.

At that moment her eyes dropped. She couldn't help noticing his erection. Quickly she closed them, embarrassed. But it turned her on more than she knew she could be turned on. If only they could be alone...she opened her eyes again. He was looking straight at her, unashamed.

He shook his head and grimaced, communicating his frustration. She noticed his fists were clenched. He was definitely warming up now. Emboldened for a moment, she ran a finger across his thigh. Lighter than a sprinting ant. Just to feel the perspiration. He was damp. She felt him shiver at her hot, wet touch.

Suddenly there was a creaking. The middle-aged gentleman opposite was wriggling into an upright position. This could be it! Jake moved a couple of inches away from the girl, but still he could feel her pulsing perfection like the rays of the sun.

The man shook his wife's arm, rousing her without ceremony. Jake watched, mouthing a silent prayer of his own and knowing that his mystery goddess would be imploring her fellow celestials for the same thing he wanted: a stolen moment to themselves.

Like a couple of unwieldy farm animals, the pair heaved themselves upright. They didn't say a word. Probably they had an implicit understanding after all these years. The wife wheezed a little as she manoeuvred her way down to the floor. The man was already standing. He nodded in the general direction of Jake and the girl. He did not appear to sense anything untoward, or feel the flames of sexual energy flying between them.

'Jeez, he thinks we're just another ordinary young couple!' Jake marvelled to himself. He knew better.

And then he forgot everything as first the man, and then the woman, walked out of the room, gently pulling the door closed behind them.

He was alone. With her. Here. Again.

Claudia no longer knew where to look. Suddenly it felt like the air around her had caught fire. What was going to happen to her now?

One thing was certain: her core was smoking right now. She could feel that longing deep inside her stomach once more. Something she hadn't quite felt for a few months. Only the heat there was even more insistent this time.

Yet how could she heed that need? Time was short. He would be roasting soon. She was expected at the dinner table in what, ten minutes? And of course that other thing: anyone might walk in. She bit her lip, frustrated.

Oh, please could she be passive and helpless? She thought she might just get away with that. Again.

He turned to her and whispered in her ear again. He didn't need to whisper any more, but God, it was sexier that way.

"I need you. I need you so much right now."

Claudia got the gist of it. Her senses swelled at his words, and she began to pant softly. Entranced, she forgot to say anything. But he would probably read an answer in her needy breathlessness…wouldn't he?

Without warning her mystery man stood up in front of her. *Oh!* His outline was better than perfect. His powerful chest, sprinkled with light hair, was level with her eyes. This was a *man* — nothing like those university boys. Claudia was captivated. Then he leaned forward, placing his hands either side of her on the pinewood bench.

She pouted. Tilted her head back.

He kissed her. Waves of hot lava shot through her body as his tongue delved straight into her mouth, gently kneading hers between her help-less, parted lips.

She tried in desperation to control herself, to listen to reason. A kiss. *That's okay.* Borderline behaviour in here, but okay. Nice. *Now quit while you're ahead.*

Oh…well, maybe a little longer wouldn't hurt. *Mmm.*

And she said nothing when he whispered in her ear again.

"I want more. Wait, I have an idea…"

What was he planning now? Startled, Claudia followed him with her eyes as he made for the door. She was drowning in curiosity, but couldn't help noticing his meaty thighs as he moved away from her.

He held the door open with his foot as he reached outside for some-thing. He gave her a peek of what it was, but she could see nothing but a rectangular outline in this light.

"*Aufguss,*" he murmured with a husky, faintly amused tone.

Claudia didn't understand at first. He was attaching something to the door, softly chuckling to himself. Then he came back inside; to her. He resumed his position in front of her, bent so his nose brushed hers.

"We will have some privacy now."

She couldn't see the glint in his eye, but she could hear it in his voice.

Oh! She got it now. The '*Aufguss*' sign. It meant that a sauna cere-mony was in progress. It meant 'strictly no entry.' It was invariably respected.

How daring! Only staff were meant to use that sign. Claudia smiled in spite of herself, inwardly impressed at his street-smartness.

Her breath hitched now. She was running out of excuses. That sign trick…it might just work! But if anyone chose to look through the window they would see it was a ruse. They could still get caught. But it was now less likely. And if they listened for the outer door opening…

"I'll take care of everything," he said. His words were loaded with assurance.

"Um-hm," she breathed. Passive and helpless might definitely work.

He took hold of her hands and pulled her to her feet.

Jake was going to do this. He'd come too far. Screw the consequences. He could not pretend to resist this girl. He was *never* going to resist her. He was sure of it the moment she'd walked through the door. She was too powerful for sensible plans to survive. Good thing he hadn't made one.

He would keep an ear open, but the rest of this was in the lap of the gods.

She was standing on the first shelf. Tall, well-built Jake was standing on the floor. It meant her breasts were directly in front of him. How could he not?

There was no part of her body he had fantasised about more than these. What was it about them? The way they made him think of strawberries and cream? God, those perky little nipples, so soft and delicate, each broad little cylinder proud and clean and clipped, yet without any in-your-face pointiness, even puckering as they were now. And each of them resting so naturally on a delightful pink bed of an areola. Twice as big as the sweet nub, no more. They were concise, all their goodness distilled into a tight, intoxicating package.

And then there was the soft, white, honey breast itself…but no, he didn't have time for this dreaming! 'Don't ride your luck,' Jake thought to himself. *Take her, quickly.*

He'd allow himself one indulgence, though.

His mouth clamped around her nipple, and he sucked. *Hard.* Claudia felt her hair standing on end and her legs widen. Oh, this was *so* good. Her stomach muscles kept on tightening, propelling her torso closer to him, as if willing more of her breast into his hot mouth.

Claudia's own mouth was agape, as now his tongue rippled back and forth across her nipple, his teeth gently resting on its base. Just a tiny nibble while his tongue roamed. The feeling was exquisite. He must be able to feel the saline taste of her building perspiration.

No way could she pretend the rising dampness between her legs wasn't there. Everything was so hot. So wet. That feeling of abandon was back. She sighed, whimpered, gave up the fight. And then forgot where she was.

∼

Jake sensed the clock ticking. Suddenly he longed for his hotel room. To have her there, with time and privacy on his side. But this might be his only chance. He still knew nothing about her. Fate might not throw them together again. Plus, this was *hot* in more ways than one.

But he knew he needed to get moving. He forced his lips away from her breast, irritated that he could not explore her properly, excite her with all the tools at his disposal, before finally having his way with her. He wasn't naturally one to hurry things. But now he summoned enough will to wrap his arms around the small of her back and scoop her off her seat; into his embrace.

She weighed nothing. He could hold her with one arm if he wanted, but wrapped both around her back anyway. Instinctively she wrapped her legs around his waist. His manhood was nestling up against her dampest place as he held her, standing upright in the middle of that far-from-private sauna.

How and where? The questions raced through his mind as he felt his erection grow even further and press against her slit. She liked the sensation and pulled him tighter with her legs. But she was waiting for his move, hanging there, patient like a koala on a gum tree.

This could work. The more he thought about it, the more he liked it. Oh, his dream would be to fuck her in the middle of the floor, on top and then from behind. Or the other way around. But here and now? Up against the wall was the only thing that made sense. From there he'd be able to keep half an eye out for intruders.

And it was starting to feel so right. The way she'd fallen so naturally into this position, the way she was wriggling *that* place against him. She was so light, nature had made her for doing it this way. And he was sensing an urgent craving from her. A craving that didn't mind doing it right here, just like this. Yielding. In his arms.

And so Jake walked with her to the door. He rested her shoulders against the wooden wall, so hot that she flinched a little as her skin, already alive in every way, touched its surface. He had her where he wanted her, up against the hinges of the door, just to the side of the little window. Her legs wrapped as tight around him as they could go.

"Listen, I can see out of the window. If someone comes, I'm going to see them."

Again, Claudia got the general idea. It sounded good. She liked that he was in charge. Now, would this thoughtful gentleman please just get inside her before someone spoiled the whole thing? She pushed her pelvis tighter against his erection, looked up at him with all the world's pleading in her eyes.

Bad Claudia was totally winning here. Big time.

She felt him move his hands beneath her butt. One on each cheek, taking her weight. It felt delectable. And he was so strong. With the wall holding her shoulders too, she could relax completely. Weightlessness was rather nice. She let her pelvis drop away again. He didn't need to ask.

She felt him bend his knees a little, raising her with his hands at the same time. What a sensation. Powerless and passive. She could let go. *But quickly now!*

He read her thoughts. The next thing Claudia knew, she was sitting astride his shaft. The sheer delight took her breath away. His hands still took her weight, but clutched more urgently at her butt cheeks now. Fuck, this weightless feeling…divine. She felt she could give everything, if only for these few stolen moments. It was so hot, him filling her deeper than she knew she could be filled.

Claudia closed her eyes as he began to thrust into her. It must take some power to do that while holding her up, she thought as she writhed and moaned. His hands were stretching her cheeks wider. It made her feel sexier, more open, more *taken*. At the same time, they helped to move her up and down in time with his own hips. She literally had to do nothing. She was strapped in for the best ride of her life.

He was beginning to find his rhythm now. Every time she was dropped onto him, and he thrust into her, she cried a little. She couldn't help it, such was the energy that went into every stroke. He too began to grunt a little with the effort.

Completely wrapped up in her own ecstasy, Claudia didn't even hear the sound of the outer door opening.

∼

Jake heard it. *Fuck!* Couldn't the nosy bastards stay out for just ten minutes? He stopped thrusting instantly, hushing the girl, ready to disengage. But he didn't.

And he wasn't going to if he didn't absolutely have to. This was brinkmanship of the highest order. He'd figure something out. From his angle, he could see through the window to the outer door opening wide. A head started to move through it, then it stopped.

Jake was reasonably confident he couldn't be seen from the outside. The coupling pair were off to one side of the window, plus it was dark. He held his breath. If someone opened this door, he was basically behind it. He'd still have half a second to throw her off him.

He could feel her breath was held too. It felt strangely beautiful, sharing the being scared and the breathlessness with her. Actually, it felt intensely erotic, her wrapped around him, breasts no longer leaving his chest because she wasn't breathing any more. So tightly pressed he could feel her little heart racing. Time stood still.

He'd never experienced a moment so tense. Russian roulette must feel a lot like this. He prayed his trick with the sign would work. He could hardly bear to look. He felt himself twitch inside her. He was still so close. A male voice in the antechamber muttered something to someone beyond the still-open outer door. Jake and his goddess stayed stock-still, suspended in every way.

Would these people fall for it?

It made no sense, she knew — but she felt safe. In his arms, she knew everything would work out. He'd made a plan. Or he *would* make a plan. So she stayed where she was, quiet and tense as a mouse cornered by a cat. Only a couple more minutes! Please!

She buried her forehead in his muscular shoulder, not even wanting to look. *Please...please don't make us stop...*

Her ears were alive again. She heard the voices in the hallway. Words to the effect that the sauna was off-limits. Then she heard shuffling. Which way was it going? Were these people snooping? Looking in the window to see that there was quite obviously *no* ceremony going on inside?

And then she heard a door click. Her heart leapt into her mouth, but the man she was riding hadn't made a move. It must have been the outer door closing again — somebody getting lost! Had the sign really worked? He was the one with the view…

She extracted her face from his shoulder and raised hopeful eyebrows. His broad grin was all the answer she needed. She smiled back, a warm, genuine smile born of shared goals achieved. Even though he'd done all the work.

"Fast!" she cried, feeling their borrowed time might be running all too low. She dug her heels into him, as if spurs were attached. Urging him. Having to stop now would be absolutely unbearable. Unthinkable.

He nodded back at her, his jaw tight. He understood. Their luck wouldn't hold a lot longer. Those people might have gone to call the staff. But it would take a couple of minutes for them to cross the garden.

He started to go again, harder. Oh, the urgency of it all was so incredibly explosive. There was something about the extra illicit spice that she really liked. She would never have put a penny on being able to come in this position, with this much pressure, this much fear. And yet…she could feel something building. And it was like nothing she was used to: this was gathering at breakneck speed.

And he was building too. She could feel him getting bigger, hammering her a little deeper and thicker as he too came close. Her cries grew bolder, his groans more desperate. It had only been, what, 40 seconds since they started again?

'The hold-up made me want it more,' thought Claudia to herself as her brain began to cloud with erotic joy again. A few more thrusts and she would be there. She was sure of it!

She thought of him inside her, of how open and taken she was, of her shoulders rubbing up against the warm wood, of his wide, powerful hands beneath her. And that was enough. She exploded, convulsing all over again as a short but intense orgasm shook her down to the very last knot in her abdomen.

He'd done it! She'd gone over the edge again! A few more seconds of seeing her shiver with pleasure and he would be there too. He looked down at her shell-shocked face and smiled at her beaming, radiant features. He loved that he was the guy behind that glow. Jake would never get enough of her, he was sure of that.

Looking deep into her eyes tipped him over the precipice. He'd thought he might struggle with the fear of being caught, but it had never been so easy. She was sexy as sex itself. He would come inside her in the middle of a busy street if he had to. Just like he was doing now, pumping spurt after spurt of hot cream into her hypersensitive, bursting pussy.

Jake only gave himself a couple of moments. *Quit while you're winning, don't ruin it now!* But not before he repeated to himself the promise that, whatever happened, he was going to get her name and number this time. He would sooner die than have no way of contacting her again.

He longed to stay buried in her all night. He knew he couldn't and shouldn't: luck could run out any minute. And the heat was getting unbearable again. Gingerly, regretfully, he pulled her off his manhood and sat her down on the bench. Experience told him she might not be able to stand just yet. Fine. But she had to be presentable, and quick.

He darted across the room and grabbed his towel. He motioned her backside off the seat and put it beneath her. Leaking all over the place would be a bit of a giveaway.

Then he took her towel and wrapped it around his waist, dominated by an erection that was still some way from subsiding. The towel just about hid it. He glanced through the window, then bent in front of her and helped wipe her between her legs. She whimpered again as he not-so-accidentally brushed her clit.

"Take your time, clean yourself, okay?" said Jake. "I'll wait outside."

She nodded compliantly, and he leaned in to give her a light, loaded kiss on the forehead before he backed out of the door.

Ever so gently, Claudia began to descend from the clouds to which her orgasm had rocketed her. She was alone in the sauna now, and struggling to get her breath back in the heat. This was no place to recover from that kind of workout. Droplets of perspiration dripped from her nose and face now.

She eyed the wall against which she'd just been pinned in mid-air and fucked. It had been so good, so right. It was like destiny had meant it to be, and that made the whole thing so romantic, so sexy. Something like pride began to well up inside her, and she could feel herself wanting to cry. She didn't begin to understand why.

Claudia resolved to pull herself together, and stayed her tears just as they began to gather. This was no time to lose self-control. For the first time since leaving the dinner table, she thought of her mother. She had to get back! The longer she waited, the more suspicious her mom would be. Or was she just being paranoid? How could this sequence of events so much as cross her mother's innocent mind? Or would she see the sated devil-girl dancing in her daughter's eyes?

She shivered a little at what she'd done. And began to worry that her flush-prone face was going to give her away somehow. Surely not — you'd naturally be red in the cheeks after leaving a sauna. She heaved a deep sigh and the warm, wet air filled her lungs. It touched her gently inside, searing her throat a little. Was she a plaything for all of nature tonight?

She looked down between her legs, self-awareness creeping up on her. He'd given her his own towel to soak up his seed — was that some kind of noble gesture? She wanted to think so. She shook her head, unsure whether to cry or smile. Cautiously she prised open her lower lips with two fingers, reddening rapidly while she kept watch for any movement through the window.

The last evidence of her wantonness seeped out of her, and she sighed with relief as she took the loose end of the towel and wiped the area clean. Then, gathering herself, she stood up. She felt a little more cum wriggle down her thigh as she did so. God, it was such a turn-on. Oh boy, she was getting *that* feeling again already!

She fought with herself, trying all she could to keep control. Quickly she folded the towel and wiped the insides of her legs once more with the clean side. She allowed herself one more eyes-closed moment, one last replay of that scene before she pushed the door to the real world open.

Then, folded towel in one hand, the naked, sweat-drenched Claudia made for the door.

Jake was waiting for her on the stairs. She met his gaze as she emerged, but she looked apprehensive. He didn't like that at all. He smiled back at her until at last the corners of her mouth began to curl into a stifled, we-have-a-secret smirk.

It was so endearing, seeing her naked and holding his towel, which was no doubt flooded with evidence of his intense, stolen orgasm. It crossed his mind never to wash that towel now. There could be no better reminder of what had passed between them than its cocktail of juices.

He was in a respectable state now, wearing his bathrobe and flip-flops. Her little blue towel was draped over his shoulder, still clean and ready for her to use. But he was shivering from the shower he'd just taken. Selfless, again.

"You need a cold shower," he said, his voice glowing with warmth and care. "I have your robe and towel ready for you. Give me that awful towel of mine. Come."

He took her by the hand and led the stunning naked blonde — *his* stunning naked blonde — around the side of the sauna hut, to the outdoor showers. She came with him, obedient.

"And then I want to talk to you," he said, taking her by the shoulders and gazing into her eyes. "We should have a drink. I want to *know* you."

To his surprise, he felt her wriggle out of the big hands.

"What is it…?" he asked, taken aback.

"We cannot…" she murmured in a low voice and dropping her eyes. "I am…I am with my mother here. She is waiting. I have to get back to her. I'm sorry. It was difficult even to find that time. I was too long."

He could see her eyes moistening. Her *mother*? What the—? How did she get herself in *that* situation? His eyes widened and his jaw dropped open. Who on earth brings their *mom*?

"Okay…" he said blankly. He had no idea what to think about this. He was completely thrown by the mother thing. Was the woman watching them now? Was she some kind of liberated parent who was about to be told everything? Of all the scenarios he had imagined playing out, this wasn't one of them. Suddenly he wanted to get out of here.

But he remembered his promise to himself. And she hadn't yet brought herself to move. She was still there, standing awkwardly in front of him, looking up with those kiss-me eyes. It took everything he had not to do it. He had to close his eyes so he could speak.

"Wait. I have two questions." He leaned closer to her ear, whispering again. "What is your name?"

She paused before answering, as if sniffing the air around him for the scent of danger.

"Claudia," she said, softly as a feather. The name oozed from her lips like running honey. Jake loved it.

"That suits you," he said. "I'm Jake."

A hand-shake didn't seem appropriate. She rested her forehead on his chest. Suddenly Jake was aware that they were alone in a shadowy part of the garden.

"Stop that right now," he smiled. "Or I will take you back inside that sauna."

As she pulled her head back up and raised her moist eyes to his, he sensed she was upset by the thought that they had no future, separated by oceans. How would she even know that? She must have picked up on his accent.

"I want your phone number," he said, gritting his teeth slightly at the magnitude of the question. "I want to see you again, Claudia. No saunas. No mothers."

She clearly wasn't expecting this, but she smiled.

"Where are you from?" she enquired.

"I'm from Canada." He paused. "But I travel here quite often on business. Every few weeks, actually."

"Oh," she said, thrown by this unexpected new information.

She seemed lost in thought.

"So…your number?" he prompted her.

Triumphantly he pulled out a pen and notebook from the pocket of his robe. Boy, was Jake glad he'd thought of that. Old-school, but steam-proof in a way that a cellphone definitely wasn't. He handed them to her.

Claudia took the pen and scrawled a series of digits.

"When do you leave?" she asked failing to hide the obvious wrench in her throat.

"Tomorrow," said Jake, his heart sinking as he told her the awful truth.

She grimaced and pouted. What could he say?

"Oh no," she whispered softly.

All was silent, apart from the distant gush of the fountain splashing away in the pool across the garden. The wind had suddenly dropped. It felt like whole minutes passed. Jake felt the need to take charge again, though he was struggling. Struggling to keep his hands off her. Struggling at the thought that he might not see her for weeks.

Then Claudia looked up him. Yes, at long last, he knew her name. This perfect woman had a name, and he loved it. *Claudia.* He would happily gaze into those shimmering eyes all night. Right here. Fuck it, she was in a hurry, not him. He took her gently by the waist. She moved closer, and spoke.

"Take me with you."

Jake was not sure he'd heard her right. "What?"

"Tomorrow…" She said it softly.

What was she getting at? She looked nervous now, and looked at the floor. Jake took her by the chin, pulling her oval eyes back to his.

"Take me to Canada with you."

It was a shy, daring whisper. Jake's heart leapt for joy.

"I'd love that," he whispered back.

The End

ABOUT JAMES GREY

He may write his erotica under a nom-de-plume, but James Grey has been widely published by magazines and newspapers around the world for the best part of two decades. He still spends much of his working life writing about topics other than hardcore sex. This includes travel books under a different author name.

Grey began writing erotica in the run-up to Christmas 2013, inspired by a recent visit to a sauna in Germany and prompted by a subsequent period of ennui at his aunt's house in France. His self-published author ego was then born on a grim, hung-over New Year's Day in England, when he uploaded *Hot Wet Touches* to the Kindle Store.

He has gone on to become a regular category best-seller on Amazon, and is one of only a small handful of male authors writing erotica. Connect with him online, and you might even find a picture of the well-travelled Grey at a book signing event.

Grey is in his late thirties and lives in a European capital city. And yes, he likes to keep you guessing. But if you want to know something, why not simply ask him? ;)

www.jamesgreyauthor.com

CONNECTING WITH JAMES GREY

I suggest your first port of call be my official website at jamesgreyauthor.com. It's the best place to learn all about me and my work — and it's the *only* place to order those coveted signed paperbacks!

To connect with my community of fans and I, Facebook's ideal. So make a request to join the James Grey Fan Group. That's where I bounce cover ideas, run reader polls, take requests and announce my news first!

I love fan mail! Just like I love constructive criticism, meeting prospective beta readers or even hearing your fantasies. You can write to me via my website contact form or email jamesgreyerotic@gmail.com.

Finally, I'd like to encourage you to join my mailing list. I'm planning some exclusive Emma-related content for my subscribers in the near future! Bear in mind too that I am at the mercy of the digital bookstores, and *they don't tell me who you are.* They could even decide to ban me overnight without warning (it happens!), destroying my livelihood and all the years of work to build up a fan base. If I have your email, at least I can find you again! For this scenario as much as anything else, won't you consider signing up via my website?

ALSO BY JAMES GREY

The Emma Series:

Escort in Training (Book 1)

Escort Unleashed (Book 2)

Her Calling (Book 3)

The Laura Series:

Out of Office (Book 1)

Playing Dirty (Book 2)

Novellas:

Hot Wet Touches (eBook only)

Hot Wet Touches Amsterdam (eBook only)

The Sex Club Diaries

Short Story Collections:

Breaking Free

Choose Your Own Adventure Erotica:

Her Desire Awakened (eBook only)

～

Access all titles and formats via jamesgreyauthor.com

ACKNOWLEDGMENTS

Oh my, where do I even begin?

I guess I'll start with you, dear reader. Thank you for buying this book — you've helped me to eat! And thanks for every like, share, review and wild raving about my signed copies. Remember, your seal of approval counts for everything in the book world.

Lori, thank you for your patience. And thanks too for all the stunning bookmarks, the grumpy 2am takeovers, those beautiful Excel spreadsheets (!) and the crisis management. I won't forget you being with me in the most troubled of times, and your sticking on my side. You too, Sharon…you deserve wonderful things, and thanks so much for inspiring me.

Debs, you have been a star for your teasers, your help with sexy cover pictures and your role as Senior Tax Affairs Officer. The IRS still makes me want to seek out a tall building every time I hear its name, but you've helped me handle it all a little better than I might have done.

Kelly, you've been a true friend and I can't thank you enough. Well done for nagging me to get to a signing – Dublin was surely the start of something! You are far too generous and kind to me, you've been an absolute blessing and you are…umm…usually right.

Thanks to all you bloggers who keep on letting the world know I exist. The online book world was a bewildering, bombarding, higgledy-piggledy place to me at first, and I've probably not communicated as I should have done. But now that I've finally started to put names to faces and figure out who *you* all are, I'm looking forward to truly knowing you.

Thanks to my parents for encouraging me to read when the other kids my age were content with chucking sand at each other. The same goes for everyone who has ever affirmed that I should write, from my first English teachers at school to my university lecturers. I have doubts about this business every single day, and you've all helped to silence them in your own way.

I must thank the dozens of magazine and newspaper editors who have published the writing I've done in other fields. You've paid me to write, and that's sent an important message about what I should be doing in life. I should also thank the editors (many of them the same people!) who couldn't answer a pitch email or take a phone call. Your silences are what led me to writing directly for my readers via self-publishing. I hope that it will prove to be the best move I have ever made.

Thanks to those who have beta-read my stories, and thanks also to Ida at Amygdala Design for some wonderful work on my covers. To my fellow authors who have shared your wisdom and experiences with me, thank you so much and let's keep doing it!

I should also thank the man upstairs for creating woman. Without the fairer sex, my life and my writing would be stricken. It seems I can never grow tired of womankind, and I cherish each encounter I have with you. You spellbind me, and I'm so glad I can put that feeling down in words for a living each day. Good job, Mr God!

More of you will come along and shower me with undeserved support, I'm sure. It just keeps on happening. And every time it does, it's a reminder that my writing makes a difference to people. Thanks in advance for those reminders. They make me carry on with this crazy, wonderful life.